Resisting the urge to throw herself into his arms, she met his gaze deliberately.

His dark silver eyes roamed her frame hungrily, and still neither of them moved. Not the slightest bit.

He was here. Alive. Safe. A feat that, as always, felt almost too good to be true...given the types of dangerous missions he went on.

"Oh my!" Retired librarian Miss Mim fanned her face while Zane and Nora continued to silently size each other up. "Is it *hot* in here or what?"

It was definitely steaming, Nora thought. But then, wasn't that always the case when she and Zane were in the vicinity of each other? Sparks flew, even as duty and honor and strong wills tore them apart.

"If this is the result of serving in the Army Nurse Corps, I wish I'd done a tour or two," Miss Patricia teased.

Not, Nora thought, if your heart had been shattered as often and surely as hers had by this gorgeous hunk of a man.

Dear Reader,

Christmas is a time of miracles—when impossible wishes are granted, and even the most elusive love is given and received.

Nora Caldwell learned heart-wrenching sacrifice as a child. She is determined her only son will not suffer the same lack of parental devotion. Zane Lockhart is a Special Forces soldier who had everything growing up. Except a purpose. He found that serving his country.

Nora and Zane can't deny their attraction to each other any more than they can seem to make their on-again, off-again relationship work. Duty and honor keep getting in the way. Zane wants to put their country first. Nora believes family should surpass all priorities.

It takes Nora's adorable three-month-old baby, Liam, and the wise residents of Laramie Gardens Home for Seniors to matchmake some sense into these two, and give them the happily-ever-after kind of Christmas they deserve!

I hope you enjoy reading this book as much as I enjoyed writing it. Happy holidays!

Cathy Gillen Thacker

PS: For information on this and other books, please visit me at cathygillenthacker.com and/or my Cathy Gillen Thacker Facebook Official Author Page.

A TEXAS SOLDIER'S CHRISTMAS

CATHY GILLEN THACKER

HARLEQUIN®WESTERN ROMANCE

Recycling programs
for this product may
not exist in your area.

ISBN-13: 978-0-373-75781-7

A Texas Soldier's Christmas

Copyright © 2017 by Cathy Gillen Thacker

Printed in U.S.A.

Cathy Gillen Thacker is married and a mother of three. She and her husband spent eighteen years in Texas and now reside in North Carolina. Her mysteries, romantic comedies and heartwarming family stories have made numerous appearances on bestseller lists, but her best reward, she says, is knowing one of her books made someone's day a little brighter. A popular Harlequin author for many years, she loves telling passionate stories with happy endings and thinks nothing beats a good romance and a hot cup of tea! You can visit Cathy's website, cathygillenthacker.com, for more information on her upcoming and previously published books, recipes, and a list of her favorite things.

Books by Cathy Gillen Thacker

Harlequin Western Romance

Texas Legacies: The Lockharts

A Texas Soldier's Family
A Texas Cowboy's Christmas
The Texas Valentine Twins
Wanted: Texas Daddy

Harlequin American Romance

McCabe Multiples

Runaway Lone Star Bride
Lone Star Christmas
Lone Star Valentine
Lone Star Daddy
Lone Star Baby
Lone Star Twins

Visit the Author Profile page
at Harlequin.com for more titles.

Chapter One

"It certainly looks like Christmas came early for you, Nora!" ninety-year-old Miss Sadie said.

Nora Caldwell regarded the ladies gathered in the Laramie Gardens community room. All were grinning and merrily nudging each other. Not sure she *wanted* to know what was causing such hilarity, she slowly turned toward the portal. What she saw in the doorway was enough to stop her heart.

United States Army Lieutenant Zane Lockhart, the love—as well as the bane—of her life. And it wasn't even Thanksgiving yet! Her knees went weak as she took him in.

Breathing a huge sigh of relief, Nora noted that the Special Forces officer did not show any new battle scars.

Clad in desert camouflage shirt and pants and utility boots, his six-foot-three-inch frame was as broad-shouldered and solidly muscled as ever. His ruggedly handsome face bore the perpetual tan she knew so well, his sensual lips the same knowing slant. It didn't appear he had done more than run a hand through the thick layers of his wheat-gold hair, but it didn't matter—the cropped shiny-clean strands looked good no matter which way the wind tossed them.

Resisting the urge to throw herself into his arms, she deliberately met his gaze, while his dark silver eyes roamed her frame every bit as hungrily as she surveyed his. And still, neither of them moved. He was here. Alive. Safe. A feat that, as always, felt almost too good to be true, given the types of dangerous missions he went on.

"Oh, my!" Retired librarian Miss Mim fanned her face, her face turning as red as her auburn hair while Zane and Nora continued to silently size each other up. "Is it *hot* in here or what?"

It was definitely steamy, Nora thought. But then, wasn't that always the case when she and Zane were in the vicinity of each other? Sparks flew, even as duty and honor and strong wills tore them apart.

"If this is the result of serving in the Army Nurse Corps, I wish I'd done a tour or two," Miss Patricia teased.

Not, Nora thought, if your heart had been shattered as often and surely as hers had by this gorgeous hunk of a man.

Oblivious to the admiring glances of the three dozen women gathered in the community room, Zane asked, "Sorry to interrupt, ladies, but may I have a word with you, Nora?" His expression abruptly becoming inscrutable, he added, "Privately?"

Where was his usual wide-as-all-Texas grin, the easy charm he managed to exhibit no matter what, Nora wondered, acutely aware he could be about to give her bad news about one of their fellow soldiers.

Oblivious to her worry, the ladies promised in unison, "Go ahead. We can handle the rest of the holiday planning session."

Breaking eye contact with Zane, Nora drew a deep enervating breath and said to one and all, "I'll be in my office if you need me." Shoulders stiff with tension, she led the way down the hall to the door just off the formal entry.

Zane read the bronze plaque next to the door. "Are you just the director, or the director of the nursing staff?"

"Both." Although she imagined he, like her brigadier-general mother, did not view her current position with the same high regard as her previous assignment in one of the premier military hospitals in the world.

He followed her inside.

Nora spun around to face him, still tingling all over. Zane shut the door behind him. Ignored the chair she offered.

She sat down behind her desk anyway.

"Why didn't you tell me what was going on with you?" he said plainly.

He wanted to talk about their ill-fated off-and-on-again romance? *Now*? Over a year after it had finally ended? With an insouciance she couldn't begin to feel, Nora waved an airy hand. "I didn't think my resignation from the Army was relevant to you, given the way our relationship ended."

Zane's gaze narrowed all the more. "How about your private life?" His square jaw jutted out. "You didn't think I had a right to know about *any* of that?"

Why was he acting so weird? Like a man on a mission? It wasn't as if he hadn't known she intended to return to the small West Texas town where she had grown up when she ended her career in the military service.

Laramie was home to her.

Laramie was comforting.

It had been to him, too, as a child, when he had left his wealthy life in Dallas and visited his much more rustic paternal grandfather's Laramie County ranch in the summers.

But now he clearly wasn't thinking about their closeness back then.

Doggedly, he persisted, "You didn't think you should at least write or call me and let me know of your plans?"

Feeling even more baffled, Nora shrugged. "Ah. Not really."

His expression changed. Became almost rueful. He sat down and leaned forward, his muscular forearms on his spread knees. He speared her with his gaze. "Did I really disappoint you that badly?"

If he only knew. Hurt filled her heart. She swallowed and tried again to explain, "I told you…it wasn't you. It was never you." Zane had been clear about who and what he was from the very start. "It was me," she admitted in a low, strangled voice. "I'm the one who couldn't handle the intensity of our affair." The fact that every time he left she had to contend with the fact she might never see him again.

He straightened, squaring his broad shoulders. "So you came here?"

It was the only thing in her life at that time that had made sense. Especially with everything else she'd had going on, familywise. "My sister, mother and I all still jointly own a home here, the one my grandparents left us." The one she had grown up in.

Nora swallowed around the parched feeling in her throat. "After serving in field hospitals and military trauma centers—" helping the sometimes mortally wounded "—I needed something low-key."

He squinted, displeased. "That doesn't explain why you didn't tell *me* about your future plans."

Actually, Nora thought, it pretty much explained everything. Sharing in his obvious exasperation, she glared right back at him. "We weren't in touch after we ended things." And hadn't been for the last year.

"Actually, Nora, *you* ended things," he jumped in to correct. Sounding a little angry and resentful now.

Guilt flooded her. "Okay, yes, I did. And I told you then that it wasn't your fault. You handled the dangerous aspects of your military service just fine. It was me who couldn't take the not knowing where you were, or what you were doing, or if you were okay. It was me who couldn't take you just showing up hurt, repeatedly, in the military hospital where I was assigned."

It had gotten to the point where she couldn't eat or sleep, or even smile when he was deployed, he was on her mind so much.

That was when he had begun to worry about her, too.

And being distracted like that, they both knew, could get him killed. So she had ended it, and a few months after that, exited the armed service honorably.

He rose and paced the office for several long moments. Stopping abruptly, he leaned against a wall, arms folded in front of him, and locked his steely gaze on her. "Okay, I get all that. What I can't fathom is why you didn't think I had a right to know!"

She huffed in frustration. Demanded finally, "Know what?"

"That you had our baby."

Zane had braced for a lot of different reactions from Nora Caldwell. Defiance, anger, resentment, even heartlessness. He wasn't prepared for shock. And dismay.

Nora pushed back her chair and shot to her full five feet nine inches. Her hair, always a beautiful chestnut brown, now sported sunny golden highlights and fell past her shoulders in the kind of loose, sexy waves military regulations never would have permitted. Beneath her elegant cheekbones, her soft luscious lips clamped down on an O of surprise, while her sky blue eyes radiated a resentment that seemed soul-deep.

Still glaring at him furiously, she propped her hands on her hips. In a pair of black scrubs, with a long-sleeved light blue T-shirt underneath, she was as lithe and physically fit as ever.

Frowning, she demanded, "What in heaven's name are you talking about?"

So. She was going to carry the ruse on to the end. Another disappointment. He'd thought she was better than that.

He met her glare equably. "Our son?"

Her delicate brow furrowed. "You and I don't have a baby!"

"Your Facebook page says differently."

"First of all, you and I aren't Facebook friends."

"And now I know why. Because you didn't want me to know about the baby."

She drew a deep breath and shoved a hand through her hair. "Obviously, you are referring to all the photos of Liam I've posted since I adopted him three months ago."

Adopted!

Zane paused. "You didn't say anything about that in any of the photos."

"Maybe because I didn't need to!" Flushing, she turned away. "Maybe all I need to know—all anyone needs to know—is that he is my son and I love him with all my heart, you dumb son of a gun!"

She was swearing at him again.

That meant she still had *some* feelings for him, right?

"Hey." Still holding her gaze, he aimed a thumb at his chest. Not ready to give up on what he had assumed up to now to be true, he shot back, "The timing fits." Too well for comfort, if you asked him. "We broke up a year ago. The kid was born three months ago."

Looking as if it were taking every ounce of self-control she possessed not to slug him, Nora nodded. "So naturally he had to be yours. Right, soldier?"

She hadn't slept with anyone else. Of that he was certain. She was as much a one-man woman, as he was a one-woman guy.

Hence, there had been only one conclusion to jump to. Still could be. Aware there was a very good reason— in her mind anyway—for him not to be named the little tyke's daddy, he folded his arms across his chest. "Let's just say that there was a definite probability."

Just as there was a definite probability their on-again, off-again relationship was about to be right back on.

Her brow lifting in disdain, she huffed, "Which is the only reason you showed up here like this! So you could do your duty and honorably acknowledge paternity!"

He wanted to say it wasn't true.

But he couldn't.

The minute their mutual friend had showed him the social media pages, he had started making plans, arranged for long-overdue leave and hopped a flight back to the good old US of A, figuring Christmas had come early for him, too.

Nora Caldwell, however, apparently had other ideas.

Ideas that apparently did not include a welcome home hug and kiss. Or anything else of a friendly nature.

She clamped her soft, kissable lips together tightly. Looked him up and down, finding nothing but fault. "I see."

Did she?

Because as far as he was concerned, adoption or no

adoption, this was their big chance. Maybe their *last* chance. If they could go back a step and start this reunion over. Something that again did not appear to be in *her* game plan.

"Well. Nice seeing you again, Lieutenant." She whipped her hands off her hips and shoved him none too gently toward the portal.

He dug in his heels. Once again, he had blown it with her, without meaning to. He lifted both hands in abject surrender. Not a usual acknowledgment on his part. "Nora..."

His heartfelt plea fell on deaf ears.

"Don't let the door hit you on your way out!" She gave one final shove to the center of his chest, and then he was standing on the other side of the portal. Her office door slammed in his face.

THE FIRST THING Zane noticed was the fact he wasn't alone. In fact, quite a crowd of senior men and women had congregated in the hallway. The expressions on their faces indicated they had heard at least part of what had transpired.

The second thing he saw was a young woman dressed like a student, in jeans and a community college T-shirt. She had a diaper bag slung over her shoulder, a baby boy cradled in her arms.

Liam.

Zane had spent enough hours poring over the social media photos, while on the flight home to Texas, not to recognize this little angel. The tiny fella was again dressed all in blue. He had a cute little face and the same long-lashed sky blue eyes as his mother. The hair peeking out from beneath the cap was light, too.

No wonder Nora had called him the love of her life.

Zane was completely captivated by him, too.

As were all the smiling seniors.

"Umm…is Nora available?" the young woman asked. "She usually collects Liam when she gets off work, which should have been about ten minutes ago. And I've got to go to class…"

The office door swung open. Nora stood there, a light jacket thrown over her uniform, car keys in hand. "Hey, Shanda. Sorry if I kept you waiting."

"No problem." With a smile, Shanda handed little Liam over.

Zane stood there. Ready to apologize again. Nora sent him a look. "Don't even…"

The circle of seniors seemed to agree it would be a bad idea to talk to her now. So, cursing the circumstances—which always seemed to be against them—Zane left.

"Well, that's a relief," Nora murmured to Liam as she ducked back into her office, gathered up their belongings and walked out to her red minivan. He cooed as she put him in his car seat. "I wasn't sure Zane was going to exit so readily."

Liam stared up at her, listening intently.

"It's a long story," Nora reassured her baby boy. Finished buckling him in, she shut the door and climbed into the driver seat. "The bottom line is, Zane would not approve if he knew exactly how and why you came into my life. He would tell me that letting someone else out of their familial obligations and adopting you was a big mistake that could only hurt me in the end. And he would be wrong." Nora drew a deep breath as she turned off Spring Street and onto Wildflower Lane, then into her own driveway. "Because I know firsthand how a child needs at least one parent in his or her life. Every day. I know what it feels like when they're not," she said, putting her minivan in Park. "And I am going to be there for you, my darling baby boy." *Whether Zane likes it or not.*

Liam chortled in agreement.

Nora grinned at her son's happy acknowledgment, then got out to begin their evening. As always, it began with a leisurely postworkday play session. She read him a few stories—on the premise that it was never too soon to start loving books—then followed that by giving him a relaxing bath. When he was cozy in his pajamas, she sat down in her rocking chair to feed him a bottle.

He drank it readily, burped like a champ and then fell asleep to the sound of his favorite lullaby. She was just about to ease him out of her arms when a knock sounded at her front door.

Wondering who it could be, she set her sweetly snoozing son gently down into his Pack 'n Play. She moved soundlessly to the portal. Opened it. And sighed.

"You again," she said.

Chapter Two

"I thought we should start over," Zane Lockhart said, capturing her gaze in that intent way that always made her catch her breath.

Nora wasn't surprised to see the handsome soldier on her doorstep so soon after their argument. She knew he'd been taught to rectify mistakes, ASAP. Whereas she'd grown up, picking herself up, dusting herself off and pretending whatever had hurt her didn't matter, because time healed all wounds.

But sadly, in this case, the passage of months hadn't fixed anything and might never.

Keeping her guard up, she stepped out onto the porch opposite him. Across the street, smoke curled from the chimney of a neighbor's home, scenting the air with burning oak.

Wary of letting him back in her life in even the slightest way, she stared up at him coolly. "And I think we should leave things as is." Frustration curled the corners of his lips. "Come on, Nora." He pressed a brightly wrapped present and a bouquet of flowers into her hands. "Hear me out."

She supposed she owed him that much, after all they had once been to each other.

She set the gifts on one of the rockers on the front

porch. Trying not to notice how strappingly handsome he looked in the soft glow of her porch light, she turned back to him and folded her arms in front of her. "I'm listening."

His expression sobered. "First, I apologize for any conclusions I might have jumped to."

About time, she thought.

He held her eyes for a long moment. His voice dropped a compelling notch. "And second, I want to congratulate you on your new son."

His words were so sincere she couldn't help but respond. Figuring peace was better than conflict any day, Nora drew an enervating breath. "Thank you."

Regret tautened the chiseled lines of his face. "I should have known if Liam were mine, you would have told me."

"You're damn right about that," she said fiercely, trying not to think how much she had always longed to have his baby.

And perversely, she still did. But that wasn't happening any more than a reconciliation, so the best thing to do was end their disagreement, and hence his reason for pursuing her.

"Thank you for coming by to say that." Nora shivered in the cold November air. "I accept your apology."

"Does that mean I get to come in long enough to see Liam again and watch you two open the baby gift?"

It'd be rude not to have him come in for a moment.

Aware she was practically shaking she was so cold, Nora picked up the gift and flowers. Turning toward the door, she led the way inside.

Acutely aware of him following lazily behind her, she glanced over her shoulder, frowned. "Why is it if I give you an inch you take a mile?"

He held the door for her. "Must be my easy Texas charm."

She made a face and quipped right back before she could think. "It's definitely something."

He had changed into his civilian clothes since she had last seen him. The tweed sport coat and light blue shirt hugged his broad shoulders and muscled chest. Worn jeans cloaked his hard thighs, sturdy Western boots covered his feet.

Eyes twinkling, he followed her into the living room, where Liam still snoozed contentedly in his Pack 'n Play.

Zane paused to regard her son with a mixture of longing and tenderness that further stirred her emotions.

Nora set the flowers on the coffee table, then perched on the edge of a chair, the present on her lap. She gestured for him to have a seat on the sofa.

"Going to guess what it is?"

She couldn't—wouldn't—make too much of this. Ignoring the faint flutter of her heart, Nora tilted her head to one side. "Something the clerk at the baby boutique in town picked out for you?"

He flashed a cheeky grin. Not the least bit put off. "I'm more invested than that."

She certainly hoped not. Because to have him invested in her life—in Liam's—was the path to heartache, all over again. Doing her best to keep her guard up, Nora undid the ribbon.

Inside the box was a completely adorable red velvet Santa outfit, complete with cap and knit booties that looked like little black boots.

Zane turned his attention to the Pack 'n Play. Observing Liam, his expression grew tender once again. "I know Liam is a little young to know what the holidays are all about, but seeing as how this is his first Christmas—" his voice roughened slightly "—I figure he ought to celebrate it up right."

Nora knew as an adoptive parent, versus a biological one, she should not be having postpregnancy hormonal shifts. But having Zane back in her life, even temporarily, was causing a seismic shift. She jerked in a quavering breath, still not daring to look her ex in the eye. "It's lovely," she murmured back huskily. "Thanks."

He reached across the chasm of space between them, clasping her delicate hand in his rougher one. "So we're good?"

Yes, Nora thought, her pulse racing despite herself. And no…

Luckily for her, she was saved from having to answer that by the ringing phone.

She rose to get it.

The news on the other end was not good.

"You HAVE TO go back to work *now*?" Zane asked.

Aware she had no time to don her scrubs again, Nora grabbed a belted cardigan-style jacket instead, looped the chained badge over her head and settled the ID between her breasts. She paused to pull on her favorite pair of Western boots. "It's an emergency with a new resident. Unfortunately, I don't have time to wait for a sitter to get here…so I'm going to have to take Liam with me."

He followed her back to the Pack 'n Play. "Is that going to be a problem?"

Gently, Nora eased her son into a fleece jacket and cap. "No. He goes to Laramie Gardens with me every day." It had been part of her employment deal, and the only way she would go back to work so soon. "I just usually have a sitter there with me. To keep an eye on him between feedings." Which she usually did herself.

"Want me to go along and help?" Zane asked.

An extra pair of hands was always helpful, particularly when an infant was on the scene. Nodding, Nora collected the diaper bag and her purse, then gathered her son in her arms. "Actually, yes, if you wouldn't mind. At least until I can get reinforcement."

Together, they hurried out to the drive. Luckily, Liam seemed more dazed than unhappy to be woken up. Not always the case.

The pickup truck Zane had driven forever was parked behind her. "I'll follow you over there," he called.

Short minutes later, the two of them were walking into the home for senior citizens. Just before they entered the doors, Nora handed Liam, who was still strapped snugly into his infant carrier, off to Zane.

And not a moment too soon, it appeared. At the other end of the hall, a determined Russell Pierce was slapping a jaunty brown felt fedora on his head. In a safari shirt, khaki cargo pants and a worn leather jacket, he bore a striking resemblance to Harrison Ford. With a physical vigor belying his eighty-five years, he was arguing with the night charge nurse, Inez Garcia. "I'm telling you, nice as this visit has been, I have to go close up The Book Nook, and then get home to have dinner with Esther and the baby."

Wordlessly, Nora directed Zane to take Liam into the community room, where help awaited him. "Hey, Mr. Pierce," Nora said, sauntering closer.

"Well, hello there, young lady!" he said. "I was just about to call you. The rest of your special order came in."

"Great." Nora smiled and gently took his arm, attempting to orient him. "Do you know where we are?"

He looked around. Suddenly confused.

"Laramie Gardens, Home For Seniors," she said.

He squinted, uncertain.

"Will you let me walk you back to your room so we can take your blood sugar and talk a moment?"

Mr. Pierce hesitated. "I still need to get home to Esther," he said more urgently than ever.

"I know you miss her and want to be with her," Nora said softly.

He nodded. Tears glistened.

Nora fought the lump rising in her throat. She put her arm through his, and together, they walked back toward his room.

An hour later, all was calm.

Nora went in search of Zane and the baby, hoping they were still in the community room. Only to hear sounds of what had increasingly become the norm.

"Yes, but it isn't fair," Wilbur Barnes said.

"All the activities are female oriented," complained Kurtis Kelley.

"We want an equal-opportunity holiday around here!" Buck Franklin reiterated gruffly.

"Hey! We gave you fellas ample time to weigh in on the scheduled activities," the always-elegant Miss Sadie said.

"You all refused," retired librarian Miss Mim pointed out.

Nora crossed the threshold.

Zane stood in front of the fireplace, a wide-awake Liam cradled in his arms. The two of them were a picture of contentment. Leading Nora to secretly wish for the impossible…

"What do you think, Zane? You've got enough distance to lend perspective," Darrell Enlow, the resident peacemaker, said.

Zane squinted at the group gathered around him. "I'm not sure you want to hear what I have to say."

"Yes, we do!" everyone cried in unison.

Zane looked at Nora. Figuring it couldn't hurt to get an outside opinion, she encouraged him with a nod.

He drew a breath, his attention focused solely on the thirty or so seniors gathered around him. "Well, when I hear you argue about whether hand-painting ornaments is an appropriate activity for guys I can't help but think about all my fellow soldiers stationed around the world right now who are away from their families, who would give anything to be home with their loved ones. In fact," he admitted, in a low, gravelly voice, "they'd be so damn grateful, they wouldn't care what they were expected to do as long as they could spend time together."

The ache in Nora's throat came back, full force.

This was the Zane she had loved.

The big, strong guy with the heart as vast as the Lone Star State. The man who never let her—or anyone else who was depending on him—down. The soldier who was always ready and willing to render aid to someone else in need.

Who was helping her out with her son, even now.

Several throats cleared. More than one resident dabbed their eyes.

"You're right," Wilbur Barnes said finally. "We can do better."

Zane shifted Liam a little higher in his arms. Her son reacted by resting his blond head contentedly against Zane's broad chest. "Which isn't to say I don't understand your frustration," he continued empathetically. "The holidays are a time when it's just as easy to think about what you don't have as it is to count your blessings."

How true, Nora thought, aware right now she was acutely cognizant of how much she had missed him. And maybe always would…

"I also know that you-all would feel a lot less lonesome if you were helping someone else," Zane concluded, his gaze softening as Liam yawned sleepily and cuddled even closer against him.

Smiling down at him, Zane stroked Liam's downy soft head.

The moment so affectionate, so unexpected, it brought tears to Nora's eyes.

Zane continued in a tone that was both pragmatic and gentle, "And I've got just the idea on how to make that happen."

"THAT WAS BRILLIANT, getting them involved with the West Texas Warriors Assistance nonprofit," Nora complimented Zane, as they walked out to the parking lot. Aware this was beginning to feel like a date, when it most certainly was not, she forced herself to put aside her increasingly warm feelings for the sexy soldier.

He opened the door for her, then stepped back to give her room to settle the sleeping Liam back in his car seat. "My family and the others running it can use the help, especially this time of year."

Nora straightened and shut the door. To her relief, Liam continued sleeping.

Tilting her head back, she looked Zane in the eye. "I know Bess Monroe, the nurse who runs the rehab unit. I'll call her tomorrow and see what we can do to set things up between us."

Zane flashed another flirty grin. "I can help with that, you know."

Awareness swept through her. Fighting the urge to touch him, Nora took a step back. "I appreciate your Good Samaritan spirit."

"But?" The street lamps brought out the wheat-gold hue of his hair.

Resisting the urge to run her fingers through the thick strands, Nora frowned. "I can't go down this road with you again, Zane." And working closely with him, on anything, would lead to just that. A fact he seemed to know all too well.

He regarded her with barely veiled bemusement. "Our relationship doesn't have to end badly. In fact—" he shrugged his broad shoulders laconically "—it doesn't have to end at all."

Nora tossed her bag into the car. "I think, given the very different things we want in life, that it already has," she said, casting him a probing sidelong glance. "In any case, Thanksgiving is tomorrow. It will be a very busy day at Laramie Gardens, with all the guests and family coming in."

"I'm guessing it won't be a happy occasion for everyone."

Nora dipped her head, acknowledging wearily this was true. For every happy heart, there would be a broken one to mend. "I'm going to need all my energy to see them through it. So we better call it a night."

Apparently not quite ready to give up just yet, he watched her climb behind the wheel. "Sure you don't need my help getting Liam in the house, or seeing you get some dinner?"

Need?

No. She could do whatever was required all by herself. Want was a different matter entirely.

"I HEARD MY dad had another episode last night," Lynn Russell informed Nora the next morning.

Nora ushered the sixty-year-old noted actress into her

private office. Although currently filming a television series in NYC, the glamorous redhead had flown back to enjoy the holiday with her dad.

"He suffered a period of brief confusion last night."

"Wasn't that the second time since he's been here?"

"In the course of two weeks. Yes."

Lynn settled in a chair on the other side of Nora's desk. "Do you know why?"

"We initially chalked the first incident up to simple fatigue. He was exhausted by the plane ride and long drive here. Neither of which is easy for someone his age."

"And the one last night?"

Nora regarded the medical chart in front of her. "We're not sure. He hasn't had much of an appetite since he moved in. So his blood sugar was a little off. We got the levels back to normal after he finished eating his dinner. And it was normal again this morning."

"So that's not likely it."

"Probably not. But with folks his age, we keep a close tab on that just the same. He could also have been sundowning a little."

Lynn turned off her phone and set her bag on the floor. "What's that?"

"It's a type of confusion that occurs later in the day. It can be an early symptom of Alzheimer's or dementia. But I've also seen it brought about simply by a change in environment in an elderly person."

"So, if it's just the move back to Texas causing this…?"

"Then his occasional disorientation will ease as he adjusts to life here at Laramie Gardens and everything becomes more familiar to him."

Lynn tapped her fingers, thinking. "And if not?"

Nora sobered. "Then treatment might be required. Which is why we have a geriatric specialist, Dr. Ron

Wheeler, coming in tomorrow morning to go over his medical records and examine him. But not to worry, your dad is in fine spirits this morning. So you should have a nice holiday together."

Her expression regretful, Lynn walked with Nora to the door. "I wish I could have convinced Dad to stay with me in New York City and continue to have home care help to assist him in my absence. But he was insistent he return to the place where I grew up and he and my mother spent their entire married life."

Together, they moved down the hall. "I can see where that would be comforting."

Lynn shook her head sadly. "He's never gotten over losing her two years ago."

Nora recalled Esther, who had worked side by side with her husband at the Laramie bookstore they founded. A kinder, more devoted couple could not have been found. "How long were they married?" She paused just outside Mr. Pierce's door.

"Sixty-three years." Lynn smiled and waved at her dad, who was standing in front of a bookcase of leather-bound classics. *Treasure Island, Moby-Dick, A Christmas Carol, Gunga Din, The Catcher in the Rye, Don Quixote*… Mr. Pierce had quite the collection. And he was deeply attached to them all.

"Wow," Nora said. "I can hardly imagine what it would be like to be married that long."

"I know." Lynn grinned as she headed in to see her father. "Not many couples make it that long these days."

Certainly, Nora thought, not she and Zane.

"Is Lieutenant Lockhart coming for the feast this evening?" Miss Mim asked.

"We invited him to attend," Miss Sadie said helpfully.

Nora cradled Liam against her shoulder, all the while keeping an eye on the dining room, where places for all one hundred and fifty residents, and the hundred special guests also in attendance for the buffet dinner at 4:30 p.m., were being set up.

Nora shoved aside her own need to see the handsome soldier. "I expect he's with his own family today."

"Ah…think again…" chimed in Miss Mim, who'd been matchmaking for the two of them since they were kids who hung out together every summer, when Zane visited his paternal grandfather.

Every nerve end tingling, Nora turned.

And there came Zane striding toward her in an olive green shirt, tie, blazer and jeans. He had a huge sheet cake in his hands. "Did your sister, Sage, make that cake?" Buck Franklin asked.

Zane chuckled. "She did. And she even put the great big turkey on it, just like I asked." He held it out so everyone could see the decoration adorning the vanilla frosting.

Nora couldn't help but compliment, "That was so nice of you and Sage." His sister was a fabulous chef, as well as café bistro owner.

Zane grinned and regarded Nora mischievously, his eyes alight with interest. "Consider it the Lockhart family's contribution for the feast today."

It was something, all right.

Oblivious to the sparks flying between Zane and Nora, Wilbur Barnes stepped in to relieve Zane. "Thanks, son."

Miss Patricia led the way across the dining hall. "I'll make room for it on the dessert table."

Suddenly, the world narrowed once again. Zane regarded Liam, who was looking around with a slightly perturbed expression on his cherubic face. "Not to worry, little fella," he said, patting Liam's head. "You'll have a chance to have cake when I bring it next year."

As if Zane would be there with them next November, Nora thought irritably. The practical side of her laid down odds he would not. Which meant for all their sakes she had to keep her guard up.

As the seniors gathered around them eased off to give them a little privacy, she nodded at the brash fabric knotted around his neck. "Where did you get that tie?" she quipped. "Pick it out yourself?"

He held out the brown, orange, gold and green silk. Then gazed admiringly at the upside-down design. "Neckwear sporting a traditional cornucopia is hard to find."

Nora rolled her eyes. "I'll bet."

He chuckled, knowing—as always—he was doing a great job of getting under her skin.

Figuring she had no choice but to brazen her way through this situation, Nora cleared her throat. She had a job to do here, and her first order of business was getting rid of him. "Seriously, it was nice of you to drop by, but doesn't your family want you to spend the holiday with them?"

Stubbornly refusing to take her hint, Zane shrugged his broad shoulders. "Mom served her dinner at noon. She didn't want any football games interrupting the family meal."

Trying not to think how much his nearness disturbed her, Nora returned, "I thought Lucille didn't allow *any* televised sports at holiday get-togethers."

One corner of his sensual lips slanted up. Dark silver eyes glittering warmly, he leaned closer and teased huskily, "I like the way you remember every little thing about me…"

She recalled way too much all right, Nora thought, flushing self-consciously.

Like the way he kissed and touched her. The way he smelled when he first woke up, or was fresh out of the shower. The way he looked at her when he thought she wasn't aware, like he wanted to hold that moment in his heart forever.

A riptide of sentiment swept through her. Followed swiftly by a physical longing that was just as intense.

"This particular memory was about your mother," Nora fibbed, lifting a nonchalant brow.

He chuckled at her sassy tone. "Yes, well, Mom's softening a bit in her old age. She allows a game or two to be on as long as we all have dinner together—uninterrupted—first."

Nora let her gaze rove over his tall, solidly built frame. Told herself she wasn't affected. Nope. Not one little bit. "Ah."

"Anything we miss, she figures can be recorded and watched later."

She didn't want to kiss him again, either. Not today. Not tonight. Not ever. "Smart woman."

Oblivious to the ridiculously out-of-bounds nature of her thoughts, Zane sighed and shook his head.

"Who, unfortunately, understands very little about the superstitious nature of sporting events. Luckily for me, the guys here *do* know how much viewer participation it takes for any team to win," he announced, grinning when Nora groaned. "So they have told me, they are all in, and will be ready to cheer on my teams with me."

Which meant Zane would be here for hours. As would she, since she was pulling a double today. It was all Nora could do not to stamp her foot in dismay.

"Just don't let things get too rowdy," she warned.

Zane grinned in all innocence and gave her a once-over that quickly had her tingling from head to toe. "Who, me?" he said.

Chapter Three

Nora didn't know what was worse. Having Zane underfoot during the Thanksgiving feast, paying attention to her. Or having him underfoot, blissfully unaware she was even around.

All she knew for sure was that he was a hit at the table he was sitting at during the meal. Even from the other side of the dining room, she could hear the bursts of laughter in response to whatever stories he was telling.

And he was an even bigger hit in the TV room, watching the football games. Enough of a man's man to appeal to all the guys and enough of a charmer to appeal to the ladies.

Luckily, she had a lot to concern herself with. Three bottle feedings and a number of diaper changes for Liam. A lot of families, and lonely residents, to speak with. By the time her second shift ended at eleven that evening, she was worn to a thread.

Aware the last football game was just about over, she decided to duck into her office and wait until Zane bid adieu to his new pals and departed. With a sleeping Liam snuggled safely against her chest in his BabyBjörn carrier, Nora sat down on the love seat in the corner of her office and let her head fall back against the cushions.

The next thing she knew she was snuggled against something big and solid and warm, struggling to wake up.

Blinking, she looked down. Liam was still snoozing in his BabyBjörn. It was to her left that…

Oh, my heaven!

She struggled to sit up.

Not easy when she was cuddled snugly into the curve of Zane Lockhart's tall, strong body. But somehow she managed. Turning toward him, she leaned forward and watched his eyes open. Refusing to get lost in the mesmerizing depths, she declared, "You can't sleep with me in my office!"

Night supervisor Inez Garcia loomed in the open doorway. "I totally agree." She shook her head at Nora and Zane. "You-all ought to go home. Pronto!"

"THERE'S NO NEED to be embarrassed," Zane said, stepping outside with her. The chill from earlier in the day had faded into an unusually balmy warmth. The night air was scented with approaching rain. "I'm sure it's nothing your nurse-colleague hasn't seen before."

Irked to find the weather shifting as erratically as her moods, Nora stumbled slightly under the weight of the baby still strapped to her chest, his diaper bag and her own shoulder bag. "That's not the point," she grumbled.

Zane reacted as swiftly as usual, easing a palm beneath her forearm, the other around her waist. As soon as she steadied, he tenderly searched her face. "You okay?"

"Yes," Nora fibbed, "I'm…"

He took the diaper bag from her resisting fingers, slung it over one broad shoulder and moved in even closer. "Barely awake?"

The sad truth.

She eased away from the hand beneath her elbow. "It was a long day." A very, very long day.

He fell into step beside her. Staying close enough to assist her if need be, far enough away not to crowd her. His every action as perfectly gallant as always.

"Let me drive you both home."

When even the gruff sound of his voice had her tingling all over? Not wise. Wishing she hadn't parked quite so far away from the door, Nora kept her eyes on her waiting minivan. "It's only two miles."

Zane tilted his head at her and Liam. "Plenty of time for you to fall back asleep, jump a curb and hit a tree."

She hated it when he was right. A sixteen-hour shift on a holiday, while simultaneously caring for her infant son, was too much. He, on the other hand, looked chipper as could be. But then Special Forces soldiers were trained to get by on very little shut-eye and still perform at optimum ability.

Using what felt like the very last reserves of her energy, she picked up her pace. "Then how are you going to get to your pickup truck?"

One half of his mouth quirked up in a smile. "I'll run back. I haven't worked out today. It'll be fine."

The wind gusted. With one hand, Nora held back the hair that had blown into her face. Maybe he did want a good run. In any case… With a sigh, she reluctantly gave in. "Fine. If you're sure you don't mind."

"I don't."

Not daring to look him in the eye, she used her firmest voice to let him know, "Once we get there, I'm not asking you in."

Out of the corner of her eye, she saw him shrug, his expression inscrutable. "Not asking you to."

She turned her head to face him. They locked gazes.

Damned if he didn't look serious about that, too.

With a sigh, Nora traversed the last ten feet to her minivan. Unlocked it via the keypad, then handed him her keys at the same time Liam finally woke.

Her little angel was not happy about being eased out of his cozy baby carrier, and into his car seat. He let his discontent be known with loud howls all the way home. And Liam was still crying furiously as Zane unlocked her front door.

"How can I help?"

Stubborn pride made her want to refuse. However, three months of experience had taught her self-reliance only took a new mom so far. If she wanted Liam to be as happy as possible, and she did, she had to let others assist her in situations like this.

With a reluctant sigh, she asked, "Do you know how to change a diaper?"

"Yep."

She regarded Zane skeptically. She knew they did not cover that in the military training he'd had.

His expression deadpan, he explained, "I've got five nieces and nephews in the infant and toddler stage. Three brothers, a sister and various in-laws, none of whom are shy about asking me to lend a hand when I'm in town."

Which probably meant he knew a lot more than she had given him credit for. "Okay then," she acquiesced, watching while he followed her and Liam across the threshold.

She paused to hand over her squalling son. "The nursery is upstairs, next to the last room on the right. His pajamas and a clean diaper are already laid out. If you can get things started up there, I'll warm a bottle for him and be right up."

Liam, who had miraculously slowed down his crying

during their exchange, stared worshipfully up at Zane, tears still glistening moistly on his rosy little cheeks.

She understood the abruptly spellbound attitude.

Zane had that effect on a lot of people.

Even on her.

Zane smiled down at Liam, as fondly as if he were her son's daddy. Nora's heart gave another leap.

"Atta boy," Zane soothed, running a hand over Liam's back. "We'll get you into your jammies in no time..." He headed up the stairs, Liam now quietly compliant in his arms.

Trying not to think about how nice it would be to have Zane here helping her all the time, Nora went into the kitchen. Three minutes later, she joined them.

Zane was standing over the changing table, laughing, a big, gentle hand placed over Liam's bare chest. "Nice shot, fella. You have a future as a comedian."

Nora edged closer.

Saw, too late, the damp arc across Zane's sport coat, holiday tie and shirt. Smelled the urine. *Oh, no.* She sucked in a breath of embarrassment and regret. "I'm so sorry."

"Really?" Zane chuckled, stepping back to let her take over, as promised. His eyes twinkled merrily. "Because I would've thought you would feel it was what I deserved for hanging out on your office sofa, waiting so long for you to wake up that I fell asleep myself."

Why did Zane have to possess such a great sense of humor? Take everything in stride? Even the news that this darling little baby wasn't his, after all.

Nora lifted an airy hand. Ignoring her mounting desire for him, she professed, just as humorously, "One of the hazards of raising a boy, I have learned."

He shrugged out of his sport coat, unknotted his tie, set both aside. "You've taken incoming, too?"

"Oh, yeah. The worst time was my first day back at work when Liam was six weeks old. I was trying to get him changed before we headed out the door. And bam, he hit me with everything he had. I ended up having to completely change both of us."

While she finished dressing Liam, Zane unbuttoned the first couple of buttons on his shirt and rolled up his sleeves. "Do you always take him to work with you?"

Nora nodded. "It was part of my condition for returning so early, that I have Liam nearby. I hire student-sitters during my shift to help out with him. But I try to do all his feedings myself, even if it means I stay a little longer to finish up my work."

Overhead, without warning, a soft staccato sounded. Was that…?

Catching her frown of dismay, he confirmed, "It's raining."

Nora gathered Liam in her arms. She looked up at Zane, achingly aware how cozy this all was. How right it felt. And would have been if only Liam were Zane's baby, too.

But he wasn't. The sound of the rain overhead picked up, thundering against the roof. Nora peered outside and frowned. "How are you going to get back to your vehicle?"

Looping his soiled garments over his arm, Zane shrugged nonchalantly. "I think I can handle a little precipitation. Besides—" he held out the stained fabric of his dress shirt and the T-shirt beneath "—maybe the downpour will help rinse out some of the smell."

Nora grinned.

Only Zane would be able to find the bright side in that.

Together, they walked downstairs.

The rain came down even harder. Nora hesitated. Only a heartless woman would send a soldier home on leave out into torrential downpour at one in the morning. Reluctantly, she insisted, "You have to stay."

He shook his head stubbornly, shrugged on his damp jacket and turned up the collar against his neck. "I don't think so." Zane opened the front door.

Another wave of guilt and anxiety swept through her. Followed swiftly by a soul-deep emotion that was even harder to rein in. "But…" she protested.

Their gazes clashed as surely as their wills. His scowl deepening, he said huskily, "You'll only resent me in the morning."

She put out an arm to stop him from shrugging on his jacket. Her hand curled over the flexed muscles of his bicep and she felt a jolt of electricity skitter through her. Face flushing self-consciously, she looked him in the eye, determined to clarify this much. "I didn't mean in my bed."

He regarded her with mounting amusement. Eyes gleaming mischievously, he said, "I didn't think you meant in your bed."

She dropped her hand. "Then…"

His sensual lips formed a sober line. "I showed up at Laramie Gardens today because I promised Miss Mim and Miss Sadie and all the guys that I would. It wasn't because I wanted to annoy you."

She fought back a sigh. "You didn't."

He clearly didn't believe her for one second. "Uh-huh." Another silence fell, fraught with tension. Gently, he continued, "I came by your office after the last game ended to tell you that."

And then he had stayed to rescue her. Lending a hand, showing her all over again what a great guy he was.

Nora released a wistful breath.

Why did he have to make everything so simultaneously hard and wonderful? "So now that I have…" He released her, turned, and swung open her front door again. Another blast of wet air flowed in. A sudden yellow zigzag of light filled the sky, followed immediately by a clap of thunder loud enough to make her jump. "I'll be on my way." He stepped onto the porch.

Like heck he would. Feeling very glad he was there, despite herself, she caught his arm, her palm curving around the swell of his bicep and tugged him right back inside. "You're not going anywhere, soldier. Not in a thunderstorm."

He turned to her, his shoulder nudging hers in the process. "There's no need for you to babysit me," he insisted.

Her palm tingling as badly as the rest of her, she dropped her hand.

Rocking forward on his toes, he hooked his thumbs in the denim loops on either side of his fly. "I'll wait out the worst of it on the porch. Then go." Their eyes met and held, and another jolt of awareness swept through Nora. Letting her know just how very much she had missed him.

She hesitated, unsure.

"I'll be fine." His tone was both conciliatory and deadpan. So why was he suddenly looking as if he were thinking of kissing her again? Why was she feeling the same way?

Nora winced and ducked as another sharp zigzag of electricity lit up the sky and thunder rumbled half a second later. Wow, that was close. Dangerously so.

A fact that left her no choice.

She had a duty and responsibility here to maintain his safety, just as he'd done for her half an hour prior.

Her heart racing, she countered in exasperation, "No, you won't," she said.

He quirked a brow.

She dragged in a bolstering breath, then stepped closer, determined to try and talk sense into him. "You know how it is in Texas, Zane, particularly this time of year. This storm could go on for hours." She gave him a long level look. "There is no reason to huddle out here on the porch, never mind risk life and limb, waiting for a reprieve that might not come until dawn. I have a guest room. You can bunk there tonight." She waved an amiable hand, deciding if she was in, she might as well be all in. At least when it came to reluctantly hosting. "I'll even wash your pee-soaked shirt."

He waved off her offer of aid, then cupped her shoulders warmly. "I can do that if you point me toward the laundry room. You look ready to collapse on your feet."

She was.

"So how about you go on to bed?" he suggested, seemingly oblivious to the way the casual contact was affecting her. With another brief companionable squeeze, he let her go. "I'll start the washer and close up down here."

Had she acted too hastily? Could they still actually be friends?

Savoring the possibility, she reluctantly gave in. "Okay. Thanks."

He nodded at her, like the Texas gentleman he'd been raised to be. "See you in the morning."

His innate gallantry brought forth another slew of memories. Time seemed to be suspended. Suddenly it was just the two of them again, their only duty and responsibility to each other.

Her heart racing, she jerked in a steadying breath, inhaling the brisk masculine fragrance of his hair and skin. It had been hours since he had shaved, and the stubble of new beard on his jaw only enhanced his raw sex appeal. "You know which one the guest room is?"

He cocked a brow, his gaze drifting over her lazily. "The one on the other side of the nursery, with the silver comforter on the bed?"

Trying not to wonder if his mind was traveling down the same forbidden paths as her own, Nora smiled. They were both adults. They could handle this.

"That's the one," she confirmed lightly. "There are towels, washcloths and soap in the hall bath, extra toothbrushes and toothpaste, if you need that."

Thunder roiled, even louder.

He nodded again. "Thanks."

She felt him watching her as she headed upstairs, realizing that despite everything, even when they were moving apart, fate kept throwing them back together again.

NORA FELL ASLEEP listening to the sound of the rain still drumming on the roof and thinking about Zane. She woke to the sound of an even softer rain and Liam starting ever so gently to fuss.

By the time she had changed her son's diaper and put him in a new playsuit, the sumptuous smell of breakfast cooking filled the air.

She went downstairs, not all that surprised to see Zane standing at her stove, making himself completely at home. Bare-chested, with his jeans riding just below his navel, he looked sexy as hell. It was all she could do not to run her fingers through his rumpled hair and rub her cheek against the morning beard lining his square jaw.

HE SMILED WARMLY at her and the baby in her arms. "I'll be out of here as soon as my shirts are dry. In the meantime I thought you might be as hungry as I am."

She was.

Trying not to think how often he had made breakfast for her in the past, never mind how often they had made hot, passionate love to each other after that, she eased past him. Retrieved a bottle of formula from the fridge. "What are you making?"

He looked in the pantry, emerged with a bag of tortilla chips. "Migas."

Her favorite.

And he'd brewed coffee and poured juice, too.

This was all so cozy. Too cozy.

She put Liam's bottle in the warmer, still cuddling her son close, then looked out the window at the water pouring down.

He followed her glance. "Yep, it's still raining."

She had hoped it would have stopped by now, but that did not look very likely, given the gloomy skies overheard.

Zane cast a glance at her drenched shrubbery and lawn. "No thunder, though." He beamed as Liam offered him a toothy grin. Reaching out, he gently touched her son's cheek. Liam chortled softly in response.

Zane slid his little finger into her son's tiny fist.

Liam held on tight.

The way Nora wanted to hold on...

Oblivious to her forbidden thoughts, Zane regarded her son, then lifted his glance to meet her gaze. "I forgot to ask you last night. Do you have to work today?"

Acutely aware of how wonderful it would have been if Liam had been Zane's child, Nora shook off her wistful mood. She swallowed around the sudden parched feeling in her throat and forced herself to meet Zane's eyes. "No. I've got the day off."

Liam jerked on Zane's hand. Grinning at the mingled demand and curiosity in her son's baby blue eyes, Zane stepped closer still. His smile widened as Liam chortled happily.

Zane nuzzled Liam's knuckle, eliciting another happy gurgle, then smiled again and turned his attention back to her. "Any plans?" he asked, that charismatic intensity solely focused on her now.

He smelled like toothpaste and soap. And pure, primal man.

Blushing at the memories the tantalizing fragrance elicited, Nora turned her attention away from Zane and plucked the bottle out of the warmer.

Working to corral her escalating feelings, she sat down at the table to feed Liam. "My sitter is coming at ten o'clock. I was going to go get a Christmas tree, but with it raining, I don't know that it's the best time to try and pick one out. I wouldn't be able to bring it inside until it dried out anyway, so I'll probably get a jump on my holiday shopping instead."

Still listening, he crumbled chips in his fist, and stirred them into the pan of scrambled eggs and cheese.

Nora drew a deep breath as the Tex-Mex aroma filled the room. "In any case, not to worry," she continued, giving him a look to let him know this meal would not be followed with the usual passionate lovemaking. "I can drive you over to get your pickup truck and drop your jacket off for cleaning on the way."

Zane flashed a sexy smile. "Actually, I'll take care of the dry cleaning if you do me a favor." He spooned up a plate of migas and a side of salsa, and carried both over to her.

Curious, she met his eyes. It was unlike him to drive a bargain. Usually he gave, then walked away. Thereby keeping control of the situation. But now he clearly wanted something from her. Something he seemed unsure she would be willing to give.

Aware this was a first, she looked at him, waiting.

He grabbed his breakfast and sat down opposite her, their knees touching briefly beneath the table. Then, his emotions suddenly as fired up as hers, said, "Come out and see the ranch my father left me in his will. And give me your unvarnished opinion about what you think I should do with it."

Chapter Four

Nora told herself the only reason she was following Zane out to his ranch was because she was interested in seeing exactly what he had inherited from his late father.

Well, that, and it had been a good way to get the sexy soldier out her door, back to his pickup truck and on his merry way as fast as possible. Before she started wanting to make love with him again… Which, she promised herself resolutely as she followed him out of town in her minivan, she most certainly did not.

Being completely alone with him without her son as an emotional shield, however, proved more challenging than she had expected. Luckily, they had the No Name Ranch he had inherited to focus on.

The two-thousand-acre spread was surrounded on all sides by barbed wire fence and covered with scrub vegetation and the occasional strand of trees.

In the center of the long-neglected land, a half mile back from the road, there was a newly renovated A-frame ranch house with a raised wraparound deck. Inside, everything from the wood floor to the open kitchen-family-living area and big masculine furniture on the first floor bore the same neutral brown and gray color palette as the exterior.

Zane's king-size bed and a luxurious bath with steam

shower dominated the loft-style second floor. A lone duffel sat on the floor in the wide-open space, reminding Nora just how light Zane traveled.

She headed back downstairs, determined to stay just long enough to be polite before getting back into her minivan and heading out to Christmas shop, as planned. "Your brother and sister-in-law did a nice job on this for you. Did Molly and Chance pick out the furniture, too?"

"Actually, I told them not to furnish it, since up until a few days ago—"

When he'd learned about Liam, Nora realized uncomfortably. And jumped to the erroneous conclusion her child was his...

"—my intention was to sell."

Made sense, she noted, since he was rarely in Texas. "And property with a move-in-ready home fetches a much higher price," she guessed, shivering a little.

"Right." He strode to the thermostat and made an adjustment. The furnace kicked on with a purr.

She looked around, trying not to feel disappointed he was already on his way out of her life. Again. "Well, your stagers did a remarkable job here."

He stood, looking over at her, hands braced on his waist. "Actually, I didn't plan on doing that, either." He tossed her a fond look. "All the furnishings, down to the dishes and towels, are an early Christmas gift from my mother."

A rueful smile curving his sensual lips, he walked into the kitchen and began making a pot of coffee. "She wanted to make the No Name Ranch house so cozy I'd never want to leave."

Nora slid onto a stool at the island. "Did it work?"

His gave her a long look that spoke volumes. Finally he

leaned toward her and with an even more intimate look, said, "It's not the decor that interests me here."

Oh, dear.

She pulled in a stabilizing breath, clasped her hands in front of her and tried again. "In any case, it's a really nice bachelor pad." For whoever eventually wanted it.

He leveled an assessing gaze on her, kept it there.

"Yeah, well—" he shrugged and turned away "—my dad never expected me to want to marry or settle down."

No one did.

In fact, she was pretty sure they still didn't.

She breathed in the delectable scent of freshly brewed coffee. Aware her knees weren't as steady as she wanted them to be, she slid onto a counter stool. "So he left you the ranch as an investment?"

Nodding, Zane lounged on the other side of the island, his arms folded over the hard muscles of his chest. "And a place I could crash while on leave and still be close to the rest of my family, who also all inherited property here."

And yet Zane had still, by his own admission, been thinking of selling the property. A move she sensed the rest of the close-knit Lockhart clan would not have taken well.

The coffeemaker gurgled as it reached the end of the brewing cycle. She searched his face, wishing for some chink in Zane's emotional armor, some sign that he was capable of more than fulfilling his pledge to defend their country. "Did your dad expect you to ranch?"

With a brief shake of his head, he filled two mugs and pushed one her way. He got the peppermint-mocha creamer from the fridge and handed that, along with a spoon, to her.

"No. Dad knew I don't have an ounce of rancher blood

in me. He suggested I do something more outside the norm with the land."

"Like…?"

"Set up a skydiving school, shooting range, ninja-warrior-type obstacle course or outdoor physical fitness training center."

Interesting. Frank Lockhart always had been a visionary. With the hedge fund and charitable foundation he created. As well as his wife and five kids…

Nora took her mug and, feeling the mood inside his home had gotten a little too intimate for comfort, walked back outside. He followed suit.

The rain had finally stopped but the ground and deck were still soaked. Hence, she had to be careful not to touch or lean against anything. Especially him.

She traversed the length of the deck, overlooking the property, thinking, considering. "Any one of those ideas would work if you marketed to city slickers looking for a little adventure. Although—" she tossed him a teasing look over her shoulder "—the property would need a new moniker."

He chuckled and sauntered closer, filling up the space, making her all the more sensually aware of him.

"You don't like the one it's got?"

He shook his head, his eyes drifting slowly over her face, before returning to her eyes. "No," he said gruffly. "Not at all."

Nora looked up at him. For a guy who'd planned to sell the property, he suddenly seemed proprietorial. "How did it become the No Name Ranch?"

"The husband and wife who owned it before me were never able to agree on much of anything," he replied with an affable shrug. "Including what to call this land, which they used as a vacation-home-slash-investment. So they jokingly called it the No Name, decided they liked that better than anything either of them was suggesting and eventually even made up a sign."

"That's actually a kind of cute backstory, Zane. You could probably use it in whatever you decide to do with the property." *Even if it's just as a way to eventually sell the place.*

He moved closer. "Maybe."

Or maybe not, Nora thought, judging by his unenthusiastic tone.

Not surprised Zane wasn't interested in doing anything he saw as that frivolous, even if it could benefit him financially, Nora took another sip of her coffee. "What does the rest of your family think you should do with the property?"

Disappointment glimmered in his eyes. "Just what you'd expect. My brother Wyatt thinks I should board and train horses, like he does on his ranch. Chance wants me to start a cattle breeding operation to supply quality mama cows for his bucking bull breeding and training operation."

No surprise there. His two middle brothers were absolute cowboys and always had been, from the time they had first set foot in Laramie County, visiting their paternal grandpa when they were kids. "And Sage?"

"Thinks I should find something adrenaline fueled to do for a living, then use the No Name as a private retreat where I can recoup from my new and exciting yet somehow less risky profession."

"I like the way your only sister thinks," Nora quipped, before she could stop herself.

Zane set his empty coffee cup on the railing. "So does my mom, except she doesn't want me to do anything the *least bit* dangerous anymore."

I see her point. Suppressing her desire to protect him, too, Nora pushed on, "What about Garrett?" His brother, a highly skilled physician, had served in the Army, too, before resigning to lead the family charitable foundation.

Zane sobered. "He wants me to help separated and current military at West Texas Warriors Assistance, here in Laramie."

"Like you're doing with the holiday gift basket drive."

"Except on a more permanent basis."

"But that doesn't appeal to you, either?" she asked curiously.

Zane exhaled. "I'm happy to volunteer. But as for a career, I see myself in a more physically active role, whatever it is."

"You could join local law enforcement." They took a lot of ex-military. And Lord knew their life was full of challenges, Nora thought.

He nodded as if he had expected her suggestion. "I've got an appointment to talk with the Laramie County sheriff's department next week."

"Good!"

"Don't get your hopes up." His lips twisted. "I'm not sure that will be a good fit."

But he was looking into it. That was something he'd never been willing to do before. "You never know." He was certainly selfless and heroic enough for the job.

"No. You don't," he agreed, taking her coffee cup out of her hands and setting it aside. "And I'm going to have to do something when I leave the military," he murmured as he drew her into his arms. "So I might as well look at all my options."

Nora caught her breath as one palm slid down her spine, flattening her against him, and the other hand eased through her hair, tilting her face up to his. "What are you doing?" she gasped, way more turned on than she wanted to admit.

Eyes warming, Zane looked down at her. He rubbed his thumb across her lower lip. "Making amends with you."

Nora splayed her hands across his solid, muscular chest, holding him at bay. Not the least bit surprised to suddenly be so flustered. It happened every time they were together.

He'd come striding in and give her one of his "I can't get enough of you" looks, and she'd start feeling the same way. As if there were no one else on earth who was ever going to affect her the way he did. Excited. Enthralled. And ready for so much more. "Hey..." she chided softly, her heart already racing, as he held her flush against him, buried his face in her hair and breathed in, "I said we weren't going to make love again."

He moved closer still and her body registered the heat.

"At your place last night." He dropped a string of butterfly kisses from her temple to her cheekbone, the lobe of her ear and the nape of her neck.

As she felt the pounding of his heart, the depth of his desire, tingles swept through her. She melted against him, her insides fluttering even as she struggled to keep her feelings in check.

Grinning seductively, he slid his hands down her hips to cup her against him. Softness to hardness. "We didn't say anything about today..."

The turmoil inside her increased as his lips parted hers. Her knees went ever weaker. She jerked in another quick, bolstering breath, the kiss deepening, their warm breaths mingling. "Zane..."

Over and over his tongue plunged into her mouth, stroking and arousing. "I've missed you, Nora." His lips covered hers. He kissed her hotly, ardently. Until she kissed him back. Until her arms were wreathed about his neck and there was nothing but need and yearning, and more need...

He kissed her the way he always kissed her, slowly, purposefully, demanding everything she had to give. Until he wasn't just taking but giving. Inundating her with the heat of him, his masculine strength. Filling her heart and soul with everything she had ever yearned for. And still the clinch continued. His mouth moving expertly over hers, his arms wrapped tight around her, plastering their bodies together. And lower still, she felt the searing pressure of need. His, hers. And she gave herself over to the thrill of being loved by him once again. Then, finally, when she thought she could bear it no more, he lifted his head. Drew back. Said gruffly, "And the way you just kissed me back says you've missed me, too."

And then some, Nora thought, trembling.

"So why don't we give each other a little early Christmas gift and make love. Here," he rasped. "And now."

NORA KNEW ALL the reasons why she should say no. Zane was never going to put her ahead of his commitment to country. He didn't love her the way she needed to be loved. As if she—and now Liam—were his entire world. And given the fact that he was a soldier first and foremost, he probably never would.

But she did care very much about him. Always had and always would. And now that he was here with her again, wrapping his arms around her and holding her close, all she could think was she needed to make up for all those long, lonely days and nights. Needed to do something to assuage the ever-present fear that something would happen to him and she would never see or be with him again.

So, if that meant she threw caution to the wind once again and let him into her life for just a little while, then she would. She could worry about being sensible later. When he eventually left Texas again. As she knew, deep down in her soul, that he would.

ZANE HADN'T EXPECTED Nora to give in so easily, but he couldn't say he minded the enthusiasm she showed as they kissed their way through the downstairs of his A-frame and all the way up the stairs.

It had been a long time. Too long, since he'd had her in his arms. Too long since he'd felt the sweet give of her lips beneath his, or the soft swell of her breasts nestled against his chest. And it had definitely been too long since he had seen her naked.

Easing his hands beneath the hem, he lifted her sweater over her head. Her silky camisole top followed. Beneath the lace of her bra, her nipples jutted impudently. A familiar thrill soaring through him, he bent his head to kiss her again and rubbed his thumbs across the crests. His body tightened all the more as he felt her impatience and heard her moan, soft and low in her throat.

"You next," she insisted throatily. Unbuttoning his shirt, guiding it off, then tugging his T-shirt over his head, she caught her breath. "This is new." She kissed an angry red scar on his upper arm.

And the last time he'd be wounded while participating in a covert military mission, he wanted to promise her. But couldn't. Not just yet. Not and have her believe him. So instead, he admitted to the injury with a shrug, tugged off her boots, jeans, bra and panties, and tumbled her onto his bed.

Hand beneath her head, she struck a sexy pose. Grinned and watched him strip down, too. Aware they were probably moving way too fast—as usual—he joined her on the bed. Naked, too. "Now…where were we?" he murmured.

To his delight, she cupped him in her hand. "Right here, I think…"

Eager to please her, he shifted her onto her back and slid between her thighs. Kissing his way across her breast and belly, he mused playfully, "I think it might have been here…" Gasping, she clung to him. Determined to make it last, he caught her hips in his hands and went lower still.

"Oh, Zane…" she whispered, her response honest and passionate and uncompromising.

Driven by the same frantic need, he explored. Caressed. Loved. Until fire pooled in his groin. She quivered and arched her back. When she would have hurried the pace, he held back, making her understand what it was to feel such intense, incredible yearning.

Closing her eyes and fisting her hands in his hair, she gave herself over to him. His heart full, he savored the heat and taste and feel of her. The way she opened herself up to the moment and the passion they shared.

Suddenly, he wasn't the only one shuddering with pent-up need. Aware he'd never had more reason to proceed with care, he paused to find protection. Then, easing his hands beneath her, he lifted her, touching her with the tip of his manhood in the most intimate way. She arched against him, her mouth hungry, her soft breasts pressed against his chest. With a low moan, she wrapped her arms and legs around him, clasping him close, taking him into her, giving him everything he had ever wanted and ever needed.

She was all woman, and she was *all* his, Zane thought possessively, as they succumbed to the inevitable swirling bliss.

AS ZANE HAD EXPECTED, it didn't take long for the regrets to come. With the two of them, there were always regrets when the intensity of their passion faded and reality returned.

As their shudders faded, Nora extricated herself from beneath him and rolled onto her side, facing away from him.

He shifted onto his side, too. Moved in close enough to spoon with her. And although she didn't move away, not yet, her slender body tensed.

Outside, it began to rain again, the precipitation slamming hard against the glass. The interior of his bedroom was shrouded in a wintry gloom not unlike her mood.

He ran a hand over the silky warm skin of her hip, lightly down the delicate line of her thigh. There was only one way they'd get close again.

"Tell me what's on your mind," he urged quietly.

Nora sighed, her gaze still on the view of the ranch outside the triangular-shaped floor-to-ceiling window. "I was just wondering if your father knew about us before he passed away." She bit her lip and briefly closed her eyes. "If that's why he gave you the property here, because he knew my family home—the one my mother, sister and I inherited from my grandparents—was here, too. And he thought…hoped…." Her voice trailed off sadly.

Zane fell silent, reluctantly reminiscing, too.

Nora had come with him to see his dad before his father died, five years ago. She and Zane had been off again at that moment, so they'd declared themselves just friends.

They hadn't really fooled anyone.

Even when he and Nora were off again, their feelings were always intense. Forbidden. Romantic.

Nora shifted to better see his face. Reluctantly, he admitted, "Dad and Mom both said you were the one for me, but they also knew you deserved better than what I was willing to give you."

Which, he admitted ruefully to himself, wasn't much, back then.

He forced himself to continue matter-of-factly, "So they understood completely why you wouldn't have wanted to actually date me."

She scoffed, as acutely aware as he that they hadn't ever bothered to formally court each other. Even when they were together, it was all about whatever moment they were in. Like now. Because they knew it could all end in a heartbeat. If just one thing during a mission went wrong. So they had just celebrated the rare moments they were together by staying up all night talking and tumbling in and out of bed.

The barriers around her heart went all the way up again. "Smart parents..."

He rolled her flat onto her back. Bent to kiss the curve of her shoulder. "Hey, it's not just my folks who disapprove of a liaison between us," he reminded her wryly. "Your mom doesn't like me, either."

Nora shrugged and wiggled out of his grasp before he could sideline their argument by making love to her all over again. Rising, she bent to snatch up her clothes. "That's because 'The General' doesn't want anything or anyone interfering with my military service."

Except Nora wasn't in the military right now.

Was she getting pressure to return? The way most valued members did?

Zane watched Nora pull on her panties, slip her bra over the sumptuous curves of her breasts. When she struggled to fit hook in eye, he rose and stepped behind her to fasten the clasp. Then he shrugged on his boxer briefs.

Curious, he asked, "What did your mom think about Liam, then?"

Nora went still.

Avoiding his gaze, she put on her sweater, then her jeans.

He pulled on his pants, too.

Finally, he guessed what her silence meant. "Are you serious? She didn't want you to adopt?"

Nora turned away and drew another deep breath. "It's complicated."

He moved closer, still buttoning his shirt. "Because you're single?"

Nora sat down on the edge of his bed to pull on her socks. "Because becoming Liam's mother cemented my decision to permanently leave the Army Nurse Corps."

He watched her stretch out her long lissome legs to pull on her boots. "Your mom does want you back in the military, then?"

Nora leaped to her feet and breezed past him. "She's career Army, Zane, a woman who spent her entire adult life rising to the rank of brigadier general." Swiftly, she descended the staircase, leaving him to follow. As she reached the first floor, she tossed the words over her shoulder, "So of course she wants me back in uniform, just like my sister, Davina! But it's not going to happen," she vowed heatedly.

"You're not going to continually leave your child to be deployed, the way your parents left you and your sister."

"No. I'm not," Nora said firmly. She plucked a brush out of her bag and ran it through her hair. Tilting her head, she met his probing glance and admitted thoughtfully, "That is the one thing 'The General' likes about you, though. Your dedication to service."

He sat down to pull on his own boots. "Somehow that doesn't sound like a compliment."

Nora shrugged. "In her view, it is."

But not yours, he thought, watching Nora cover her lips with gloss, then drop the tube back into her purse, too. Hands on her hips, she spun around, looking for her rain jacket. "As for what you should do with this ranch…"

He blocked her path to her coat. Lifted a brow. He might always be departing to serve his country, but she was always shutting down discussion whenever things got too intimate or intense.

"Deft change of subject," he drawled.

Ignoring his gentle rebuke, she lifted her chin and speared him with a testy gaze. "If you want to know the truth, I think my opinion is unnecessary, because you *already know* what your plan is regarding this ranch."

Damned if she didn't know him through and through.

"You're just not willing to share whatever that is with anyone yet."

Also true.

Color flooding her cheeks, she blew out a frustrated breath. "But it should be whatever *you* want, long-term, Zane, not what *your family* desires."

On that much they totally agreed. He promised her gravely, "It will be."

"Oh, and for the record…" Still looking deliciously tousled, she waved an airy hand toward the bedroom.

"I'm not sure what this was just now, except for more reckless behavior on my part." She stepped closer, her hands fisted at her sides. "But I am certain about one thing."

"And what's that?" he countered gruffly, feeling another exit speech coming.

Her lower lip trembling, she announced with a great deal of wariness, "I can't do this with you again, Zane. This whole bit where I feel like we're really starting to become a couple, only to discover that nothing has really changed, after all."

He knew that, too. "I've already told my commanding officer that I'm not reenlisting. When my tour is over January 15, I'm out."

She surmised sadly, "But between now and then, you'll have to go back."

He helped her put on her rain jacket. "On December 27, yeah, I will have to rejoin my unit. But only for a couple of weeks."

Nora stiffened. "So you say now."

He caught her wrist before she could bolt. "I mean it now, Nora."

Hurt shimmering in her eyes, she pulled away. "You meant it four years ago, too, when you told me you were resigning your commission."

Her icy rebuke stung.

He followed her out onto the porch, where the rain was coming down hard. Grimly reminded her, "You know what it was like back then. The danger a lot of our troops and diplomats were in!"

Oblivious to the pouring rain, she shook her head. Sighed sadly. "There will always be turmoil somewhere in the world. Always someone in need of rescue, Zane."

Frustration churning through him, he folded his arms

in front of him. "Why won't you believe me?" She had to know he had never lied to her. Never pretended to want or need anything he didn't.

Looking as piqued as he felt, Nora took a deep breath and tilted her face up to his. "Because, Zane, if I know anything, it's that duty-driven soldiers like you never change." Her soft lips thrust out stubbornly. "If they did—" she paused to look him in the eye and let her harsh words sink in "—Liam wouldn't be my son. He'd still be my *nephew*."

Chapter Five

Zane blinked in surprise. "What the hell are you talking about?"

Nora passed a hand over her eyes. What was it about this man that had her spilling her guts every chance she got? Especially when she had sworn to keep the circumstances surrounding Liam's birth private!

She slumped against the porch railing, knees weak, hands clamped tightly on either side of her. "My sister, Davina, is Liam's biological mother."

Zane took her by the hand and led her back inside his house. The next thing she knew he was taking off her coat and leading her over to the sofa. Sitting next to her, he wrapped an arm about her shoulders and clarified with gentle astonishment, "And your sister gave him over to you to raise?"

Nora nodded. "Yes." It was a relief to finally talk about this with someone outside her family.

"But why?"

"Because Davina couldn't bear to leave the Army."

Zane stood and went over to light the fire in the grate. "She could have remained a military linguist and still been a mother."

"True." Nora watched the logs flame. "But she wouldn't have been able to sign up for the extremely demanding assignments she favors. Not with a clear conscience, anyway."

Zane replaced the screen, then came back to her. "What about Liam's biological father?"

"He's in military intelligence. And was no more interested in becoming a parent or leaving the military than Davina was, but they both knew I wanted a family." She sighed. "So they asked me if I was interested in adopting. Otherwise, they were going to give the baby over to a private agency, right after birth, and let them find loving parents and a good home."

Zane walked into the kitchen, returned with two fresh cups of coffee. "So you said yes."

Noting he'd added just the right amount of flavored creamer to hers, Nora took a long, enervating draught, let the beverage warm her from the inside out. "Not right away. To tell you the truth, I kept thinking my sister would change her mind. Especially when she was confronted with the reality of meeting her newborn infant for the first time. In any case, she stayed at a friend's place in Pittsburgh during the last four months, while she was on medical leave, and I flew up to be with her when she gave birth to Liam."

Sensing—correctly—that Nora needed her physical space, Zane lounged against the mantel. "Your mom?"

Restless, she stood, too. "Was in meetings in South Korea at the time."

Zane watched her pace to the windows. "So 'The General' didn't come back?"

Nora swung to face him and took another sip. "She Skyped with us. Met her new grandson that way. And told us both we were doing the right thing."

Zane gave her a bluntly assessing look. "Davina wasn't upset by your mother's absence?"

Strangely, no. Nora shrugged and with a great deal of effort met Zane's penetrating gaze. "She didn't want to make a big deal over Liam's birth, either. Although they were both happy for me."

"And that was it? Davina didn't have any second thoughts? Then or since?"

The unselfish part of Nora only *wished.* "She loves him like a distant aunt. That's all. Davina's real passion is for her work with the Army, just like my mom. Everything else pales in comparison."

Zane ambled over to join her at the window. Gently caressed her cheek, then said philosophically, "Sounds like Liam may have dodged a bullet, then. 'Cause it's clear you adore him."

At the mention of her son, Nora's heart filled with love. "I do."

"I can see why." Zane's lips curved into an empathetic smile. "He's a really cute little fella."

Another silence fell and they walked back into the kitchen. Zane offered Nora more coffee. Declining, she drained her mug and put it in the sink. He set his mug next to the coffeemaker.

"What was your mom's reaction to becoming a grandmother?" He was standing so close she could feel the heat emanating from his powerful body.

Nora shrugged, doing her best to hide her deep disappointment about this, too.

She couldn't help but compare her every-woman-for-herself family to Zane's much more close-knit brood. To her consternation, he seemed to be doing the same.

"As usual," she replied, standing with her back to the counter, her arms clamped in front of her, "The General was more concerned about the *logistics* of care than the emotions involved." She sighed wearily. "From the first, she wanted to ensure that our duty and responsibility to the new life was met. A solution found that would best suit all of us."

Zane regarded her sympathetically.

Aware he was going to be very hard to resist if he kept caring for her this way, Nora replied matter-of-factly, "It was actually her idea that I take over the familial obligation and raise Liam myself."

He moved closer still and lounged next to her. "Like your grandparents brought up you and your sister in your parents' absence."

Nora nodded, aware that although she had never lacked for love from her mother's parents, she had acutely missed the day-to-day attention of her own.

His expression turning even more serious, Zane pivoted to better see her face. "And Davina was on board with that idea, too?"

Nora nodded, lifting her chin to meet his empathetic gaze. "She was the one who wanted to take it a step further, make it official and have me actually *adopt* Liam."

Zane did not appear surprised by any of this. Maybe because he knew both her sister and mother, and how unmaternal they both were. He walked over to pour himself the very last of the coffee. "So Davina would be clear of any future parental responsibility?"

Reluctantly, Nora admitted, "That, plus Davina knew how hard it was for us kids, having parents who chose active duty over us, year after year after year. Even when Dad died in that training accident, when we were in our teens, Mom refused to request in-country assignments. She was on track to be brigadier general. And nothing was going to stand in her way of achieving her goal."

Nora fought the tide of emotion rising inside.

Swallowing hard, she forced herself to continue, "The

General envisions the same bright future for Davina, if she stays on track. And my sister intends to do just that. Now that this 'blip' in her rise to success has been dealt with, anyway."

Zane's gaze narrowed, his expression grave. "Is any of this common knowledge?"

"No. Davina and my mother were both afraid if word got out, some of her fellow soldiers would think less of her, and it would hurt her chance for promotion, and garnering the plum assignments she has come to really enjoy."

"Like being the assigned interpreter for some of the top brass, overseas?"

Her breath hitched in her throat. "Right."

Zane leaned over to put his empty mug in the sink, next to hers, his broad shoulder brushing hers in the process. "And you agreed with this part of the plan, too?"

That was much harder to quantify.

Noting the rain was diminishing once again, Nora confessed, "I want to protect Liam. Make sure he feels safe and loved and wanted and has the kind of good, stable home every child deserves."

He straightened slowly, his big body blocking any easy exit she might have made. "Are you ever going to tell him the truth?"

Nora raked her teeth across her lower lip, shivering as Zane tracked the movement. "When he is a lot older, if need be. If, on the other hand—" *as I really hope* "—Liam demonstrates no curiosity about what his biological origins were, then…" She let her voice trail off.

Zane clamped a hand on the counter on either side of her. His expression turning even more brooding, he said, "Okay, I get why you did what you did for the little guy, even if you've put yourself at risk for tremendous heartache down the road."

Nora stiffened, wanting to deny the potential for hurt was there. She couldn't—not in good conscience, anyway. So she met his gaze, aware her emotions still felt pretty raw. "If you're worried the adoption won't become final in three months…"

Apparently, he was.

With a short exhalation of breath, she flattened a hand over the center of his chest and slipped out of the cage of his arms. "You needn't be. Davina is not going to say one thing only to later do another."

Zane shot her another intuitive glance. "Why do I suddenly think you're comparing me to your sister?" he asked, deadpan.

Maybe because she was?

He waited. Expecting—no, *demanding*—she explain what she was thinking and feeling.

Deciding far too much soul-baring had been done for one day, however, Nora went in search of her coat and bag once again. "Look, I get it, Zane," she said over her shoulder. Then she swung back to face him.

"I've even felt a tiny fraction of what you and my mother and my sister and a whole host of other soldiers feel about putting your service to your country above all else. Including family. And it's admirable, I know." Aware she was suddenly on the verge of tears again, she shrugged on her rain jacket, lifting her hair out of the collar, then zipped it up. "Because without people like you the world would be a much less safe place for the rest of us."

Once again, he saw far more of what she was thinking and feeling than she would have wished.

Shoulders stiff with tension, Zane walked her to the

foyer. "Except you'd never turn your back on loved ones in order to go off and rescue someone else."

She opened the door, then paused in the portal. With difficulty, she met his probing gaze. "I'm not sure I'd put it quite that way," she returned. "But you are right. Now that I have a son I love more than life, I couldn't leave him behind for weeks and months at a time for any endeavor, no matter how noble."

She paused to let her words sink in. Ignoring the telltale wrench of her heart, she added resolutely, "Liam has to come first. Ahead of my work. My duty to others. And most definitely my personal life, Zane."

He studied her with a look that was maddeningly inscrutable. Finally, he palmed his chest. "So where does that leave us?" he asked gruffly.

Nora drew a deep breath, her emotions in complete turmoil once again.

If only Zane were going to be around for more than a few weeks. But he wasn't, so...

She threw up her hands in dismay. "I don't know, Zane. I'm going to have to think about it."

"SO WHAT DO you think, Liam?" Nora cooed late Saturday morning, as she situated her son in his stroller, a short distance away from the driveway.

The previous day's torrential rain had left the Texas skies sunny and clear and briskly cold.

"Are you ready to see Mommy take our Christmas tree off the roof of our car?"

All bundled up, Liam gurgled happily.

"Then here we go!" Nora said.

The only problem was that the twine the lot attendant had secured it with was awfully tight. So tight, it was hard to get the utility scissors between the metal and pine. But finally she managed and with a sigh of relief, grabbed on to one of the thick branches and gave the tree a tug. It didn't budge at all.

She turned to see what her son was doing. He had his head tilted to one side, a cloth-covered rattle clutched in one hand. "I'll get it," she promised cheerfully.

Figuring it might go easier if she snipped the twine on the other side, too, Nora walked around. Cut again. To no avail.

The big tree still wouldn't budge from the center of her minivan roof.

"Need a hand there, darlin'?" The deep masculine voice sent a thrill up her spine.

Nora turned to see Zane jogging up the sidewalk toward her.

It wasn't surprising he was out for a run. Active duty military worked out daily. Nor was she surprised that he was on her street. He could run up and down every avenue, business or residential, in the town limits and still barely get in his usual six miles. What was disconcerting, however, was just how happy she was to see him. They'd only been apart twenty-four hours, yet it felt like so much longer.

Especially because they'd left things so up in the air.

He squinted, grinning, awaiting a response.

Embarrassed not to be able to handle this chore by herself after all, she came back around to see Liam, who was still watching patiently. Then she decided, why look a gift horse in the mouth? "Sure," she told him, "if you think you can get it down."

He reached over the minivan roof. Tall enough to grasp the center of the evergreen, he lifted it up and over and down, standing it upright. It was a foot and a half taller than his six foot three inches and almost twice as wide among the lower branches as his extended arm.

He gave it an admiring glance. "Nice tree."

As well as a fair sight bigger than she'd realized. But that was okay, she thought, since her home had high ceilings.

His gaze drifted fondly over her. "Do you have a stand for it?"

Nora felt an answering warmth. "Inside."

"I'll carry it in for you."

The assumption she couldn't handle that, either, rankled almost as much as her ever-resurging feelings for him. She wanted to be friends with him, at the very least, but she wasn't sure she could limit it to that. And that could mean trouble. For both of them. "I've got it," she announced cavalierly.

He lifted a brow. "Sure?"

Reminding herself she had decided to take a time-out to decide what kind of relationship they should have in the future, she nodded and grabbed hold of the middle of the tree. He made sure she had it, then let go.

The weight of it sent her reeling backward.

He caught it with one hand, her waist with the other, then flashed the kind of wolfish grin that said he always knew best. "Why don't you let me give you a hand?" he asked quietly.

Figuring the fastest way to have him on his merry way was to acquiesce, Nora drew a deep breath. "Thank you." Spine stiff, she extricated herself from his protective grip. Taking hold of Liam's stroller, she led the way to the door and put her baby boy inside, in the corner of the living room, well out of harm's way. Then went back to hold the door for Zane.

He carried the tree in and over to the stand.

Short minutes later, it was upright and secured into the bottom of the base. Unfortunately, it practically scraped the ceiling with its height. And was clearly bigger and fuller on one side than the other. Flushing, Nora turned the evergreen one way, then the other. To no avail. It still looked almost-comically lopsided.

Grooves deepened on either side of his mouth. "You could put it in a corner with the skimpy side hidden from view," he suggested. "That's what my mom always does."

"Lucille has this problem?" Hard to imagine. His mother was so elegant, so pulled together. Competent in all the cozy nesting ways her own mother was not.

"You can never really tell what you're getting on the lot, with all the trees bunched together like that. That's what makes it fun." Zane moved the tree around. "See?" He pushed it back. "It looks fine now."

Surprisingly, it did. If you didn't look too closely, that was.

From his stroller, Liam kicked his feet and gurgled happily, albeit a little impatiently.

Aware what was really important was finding a way to embrace the Christmas spirit and do everything in her power to make her son happy, she turned back to Zane.

Perhaps their next step was to simply try and be friends... "Want to stay and help us decorate it?" she asked impulsively.

Regret flashed in his eyes. "Love to." He hunkered down to fondly brush her son's cheek. "Just can't do it today. Which is why I came by."

He straightened to his full height, his tall, physically fit frame towering over her more petite one. He regarded her for a long careful moment.

"I need to talk to you about the gift baskets for soldiers."

"Okay." Nora ignored the sudden racing of her pulse.

"Miss Mim and the others wanted to help with that, but if the presents are going to make the next transport, the Army needs them by Monday noon. So we're going to have to get them all put together tomorrow afternoon. Is that going to be doable on your end?"

"Sure," she replied, knowing there was nothing her senior patients liked more than still feeling needed. Working to hide her disappointment she and Zane wouldn't be spending any more time together today, she moved close enough to inhale the lingering woodsy scent of his aftershave. "How many gift baskets are we talking about?"

"West Texas Warriors Assistance has pledged to provide ten thousand."

Nora staggered dramatically backward, a hand to her heart. Zane laughed, as she meant him to.

"Not to worry." He grasped her wrist lightly and reeled her back to his side. "We've got four churches, three civic organizations and a big group of high school students working, too. So if Laramie Gardens can't handle their allotment of a thousand," he said, letting her go once again, "some of the other organizations can pick up the slack."

Oblivious to the way her skin was still tingling from his touch, Zane sobered. "Just let me know what to expect, so I can make sure the supplies are all where they should be by the time we get started."

She nodded, doing her best to concentrate on the requisite logistics instead of the ruggedly handsome man opposite her. "I think we can do it." Nora walked over to get her son out of the stroller. "When will you be bringing the stuff by?"

"Just before we get started tomorrow. I'm heading to Dallas and Fort Worth with my brothers and a few other

WTWA volunteers shortly to pick up a lot of the donated materials."

Once again, she had to work to hide her disappointment. She tore her eyes from the sinewy contours of his chest. "Then Liam and I won't keep you," she promised.

Even if she, at least, really wanted to. Even if he had only twenty-seven days of leave left.

Not, she reassured herself firmly, that she was counting.

Chapter Six

"Okay, does everyone understand what we're doing?" Zane asked the one hundred seniors assembled in the Laramie Gardens dining hall, the next afternoon. "Everyone has five baskets in front of them, and some sheets of red tissue paper that you can use to line the bottom."

He turned to Nora and waited for her to demonstrate. Trying not to notice how sexy he looked—both in and out of uniform—she did.

"While you're all doing that, we'll come around and pass out the items that go in the baskets." He walked over to hand her the items. "Then we'll put the holiday cards the elementary school kids made for the soldiers on top of that." Their hands brushed as he gave her one. "And wrap the baskets."

Intoxicated by his genial, take-charge nature, Nora again showed the seniors how to proceed. Securing the cellophane overwrap with a snap-on bow.

Smiling, Zane turned his attention back to the crowd. "Once we finish the toiletries gift baskets, we'll start on the food ones and use the same process. Okay?"

Resident Kurtis Kelley cupped his hand around his mouth. "We got it, Lieutenant! So get moving already!"

Everyone laughed.

Zane took a pushcart. The younger volunteers he'd

brought with him to help out—mostly ex-soldiers and their wives or husbands—followed. Nora took up the rear.

Perhaps because it was so well organized, the process went remarkably fast. Three hours later, each senior had put together ten gift baskets. The younger volunteers put them in shipping boxes, which would then be loaded onto trucks.

Yet few seemed ready to disperse as they filtered out into the community room while dinner was being set up by the kitchen staff. Nora didn't want to leave, either, with Zane still there. So she retrieved Liam—who was still sleeping soundly in his stroller—from his sitter and returned to find the handsome soldier standing next to the fireplace, holding court.

"So tell us, Lieutenant, did you always want to be in the Special Forces?" Miss Sadie asked.

Interested in the answer, too, Nora parked the stroller in a distant corner of the room and took a seat next to her son.

Zane lounged against the mantel and shot her a surprisingly intimate look, which caused her to blush in return. "I definitely wanted to do something adventurous."

"Because your grandfather was career military?" Miss Mim pressed.

Several people turned to see what had so thoroughly captured Zane's attention.

He let his gaze drift over Nora one last time, before turning back to the crowd. "That, and the fact I had so many conditions put on me while I was growing up. For example—" one half of his sensual lips crooked up ruefully "—I was permitted to jump out of an airplane, but only once, on my eighteenth birthday, and only with a skydiving instructor of my parents' choosing. After much instruction."

Miss Patricia scoffed. "Sounds kind of reasonable."

Zane frowned, the way he always did when he felt boxed in. "From their point of view, maybe. Not mine. By the time I was sixteen, I was already visiting a recruiter."

Nora remembered. Even as a kid, Zane had been determined to one day be the kind of person who made a real difference in this world. He still was, she thought admiringly.

"The sergeant took one look at my grades and convinced me I had what it took to be in the officer corps and lined me up with a ROTC scholarship at the college of my choice, which happened to be the University of Hawaii Warrior Battalion."

Grins all around. Kurtis Kelley mimed the hula. "Because of all the pretty island girls?"

Nora rolled her eyes, recalling how jealous she had been then. For no reason, it had turned out. Zane only had eyes for her, and she him.

"Well…" Zane drawled with a flirtatious wink that had the ladies tittering. "That, and it seemed like one of the most challenging programs to get into and graduate from. And I thought it might be fun to learn to surf while I was in college."

Everyone chuckled again.

Moving to stand closer to Nora, Zane related casually, "And then of course, once I was in, I had to go for the maximum challenge, the Special Forces."

The former town librarian, who'd known them both as kids, looked from Nora to Zane. "Any regrets?" she asked him.

Getting Miss Mim's point, Zane's eyes briefly met Nora's. He knelt down to protectively survey the sleeping Liam. "Not about my chosen career, no."

Silence fell.

She had the feeling Zane was about to ask if she needed any help getting Liam home, when the vivacious and no-nonsense Betty Blair asked, "Nora, why did you go into the Army Nurse Corps?"

"To please my mother and honor my late father."

"And...?" Miss Sadie pressed.

Nora shrugged. Determined to lighten the mood, she quipped, "Ah...take care of the men who love danger?"

Everyone laughed again.

"How come you didn't marry one of them while you were in the corps?" Kurtis Kelley asked.

Dear Lord, how had they gotten into this? "It's complicated," she said, squirming uncomfortably.

Zane tilted his head to one side, amusement curving his lips. He aimed a thumb at the center of his chest. "I'd like to hear more," he said, a wickedly sexy gleam in his dark silver eyes.

Not surprisingly, from the women in the room, there were swoons all around.

Figuring if she didn't put a stop to the matchmaking now, they'd be producing strands of mistletoe at any minute, Nora drew a breath and set everyone straight. "The truth is, I've never wanted to date anyone who was actively serving in the military, because I grew up with two parents who were always deployed, and I don't like being left behind all the time."

The quizzical regard in the room deepened.

"I find it difficult to believe a woman like you didn't revere your fellow soldiers' commitment to country, honor and duty," Buck Franklin scolded.

That was the hell of it.

Nora nodded, accepting the criticism. "The noble part of me did value that then, and I still do." She turned to look at Zane, wanting him to understand this much, even if it hurt his opinion of her.

"It was the selfish side of me that felt abandoned and distraught every time someone I cared about was deployed. And believe me—" she held up a staying hand, confessing, even as guilt racked her soul "—I know that's wrong. And that in turn makes me feel like I've hurt and betrayed them way more than they've ever hurt me by leaving."

There was a murmur of understanding from the women in the room. The men, however, seemed to struggle with her candid revelations.

Turning away from Zane, and the sharp rebuke in his expression, Nora pushed on, "Plus, I knew those kinds of emotions weren't something any couple could build a life on. So I tended not to go there in the first place."

Or at least she had *tried* not to go there.

Zane had managed to cut through her barriers time after time after time.

Often to their mutual regret.

Which was why they had been off-again as much as they had been on-again.

"Surely, some of the men must have asked you out anyway," the hopelessly romantic Miss Sadie persisted.

All eyes turned expectantly to Zane.

"I won't say she wasn't chased. And chased with enthusiasm." Zane comically waggled his brows. "But she was hard to get."

Recalling exactly what he was talking about, Nora flushed.

"I bet you could have won her over if you tried," Betty Blair insisted.

Zane shrugged and reached out to affectionately pat Nora's shoulder. "Actually," he conceded playfully, to all, "I'm still trying."

"WHY DID YOU have to say that in there?" Nora chided, the moment they retired to her office.

Zane shrugged, refusing to apologize for publicly staking his claim on her. "First, it's true." Hands shoved in the pockets of his jeans, he ambled closer. "Second, everybody here knows I have a thing for you. And vice versa."

Her heart skittering in her chest, Nora drew in another whiff of his tantalizing aftershave. "How could they know that?" she demanded as she set the brake on the stroller.

He flashed a mischievous grin. "The way you look at me and the way I look at you."

Heavens! Nora knelt down to remove her son from his stroller. She handed Liam to Zane to hold, then went to get the diaper bag. She moved to set up a changing pad on the love seat. "You are incorrigible—you know that?"

Zane pressed his cheek against the top of Liam's downy soft head. "This little guy doesn't seem to think so."

The sight of her son cuddling contently against Zane's broad chest generated a wave of warmth.

"You're right," she admitted softly, watching Liam gaze adoringly up at the lieutenant. And Zane return the affection tenfold.

If only the two had been father and son! How wonderful would that be?

But they weren't, so…

It was time she came back to Earth.

Nora cleared her throat. Fresh diaper out and ready, she reached for her son.

As Zane carefully handed him over, Nora looked into his eyes, serious now. "Thank you for involving our residents in the charity work today. It really helps them to feel needed and appreciated."

He lingered close by while she changed her son. "It was my pleasure. So what next? When do you get off work?"

"Two and a half hours ago," Nora admitted ruefully, putting her baby boy in his fleece jacket and matching powder blue cap.

Although she could have left, she'd wanted to stay and lend a helping hand with Zane's charity project, too.

He sent her an admiring glance. "Got any plans for dinner?"

"Not yet." Nora stood and handed off Liam once again, so she could put her own coat on. "I'll figure something out after I get this little guy fed and in bed."

He shifted his gaze to her lips. "Want to figure something out together?"

She felt herself floundering. "Um…I can't go out tonight."

He came closer. "I'll bring something in."

The idea of not having to cook was almost as irresistible as the notion of spending the evening with him. Yet there were inherent dangers in doing so, too.

She could fall for him all over again.

Be tempted into making love with him again.

Thereby paving the way for even more brokenheartedness than they had already suffered at each other's hands.

They could also become strictly platonic friends.

Learning how to enjoy each other's company without passionate complications.

The amorous look on his face indicated that was a long shot.

She grinned and shook her head. "You are persistent."

He winked flirtatiously. "And you're resistant."

Nora groaned at his play on words.

Brushing the back of his hand across her cheek, he bent to kiss the top of her head. "That doesn't mean we can't have a good time together, sharing a meal."

He seemed serious now, in the way that meant he wanted the two of them to get closer. The heck of it was she wanted that, too.

Zane held the door for her. He accompanied her and Liam as they walked through the foyer and out into the fading light. "So is that a yes, or a maybe, or a…?" His voice cut off abruptly.

Nora paused at what they saw, too. Mr. Pierce wandering through the cars, before stopping next to her minivan, one hand on his thinning silver hair, the other rested on his waist. To her dismay, the older gentleman wasn't wearing his leather jacket or his fedora. He also looked perplexed, and then some.

"Problem?" Zane guessed.

"I don't know." She handed her son over to him. "Would you mind coming with me, just in case…?"

"Sure."

"Hi, Mr. Pierce!"

The older gentleman turned. "Nurse Nora!"

Nora sighed with relief. Thank goodness he knew who she was! She strode cheerfully toward him. "What are you doing out here?"

"Actually—" Russell Pierce massaged the back of his neck thoughtfully, watching as she removed her car keys from the outside zipper pocket on her bag "—I'm not sure. I know I came out here for something…I just can't recall what."

"That happens to me all the time," she said lightly.

With the keypad, she electronically unlocked and opened up the side door.

She paused to put her purse and Liam's diaper bag inside the cargo area. "I run up the stairs at home looking for something, then get up there and can't for the life of me recall what I was going to get and run back down the stairs, only to remember what I was going to get."

Mr. Pierce chuckled.

Zane chimed in, "I think it happens to all of us."

"I imagine so." Mr. Pierce turned back to her vehicle and ran his hand over the gleaming red surface. "Is this your minivan?"

"Yes, it is."

"It's a beauty. Esther and I had one just like it. We got it a couple of years before she passed." He paused affectionately, reminiscing, "She used to really love driving it, and so did I."

"I can see why." Nora and Zane both smiled. "I love mine, too." Aware the elderly resident was shivering without his coat, she slipped her arm through his.

"I still can't figure out why I came outside, though," he said, perturbed.

Nora patted his arm gently. "I'm sure it will come to you later. The way it always does me. Usually when I least expect it!"

They all chuckled.

She regarded Mr. Pierce intently. "In the meantime, they've started serving dinner in the dining hall. And I know you don't want to miss that."

"No, I do not," Russell Pierce said with enthusiasm. "Fried chicken, isn't it?"

"With all the trimmings. Is it okay if I walk in with you?" Nora asked, still holding on to his arm. "I think I left something in my office."

She handed her minivan keys over to Zane, suggesting cheerfully, "If you want to get the heater running..."

He nodded at her, looking completely natural with her baby boy in his arms. "No problem."

By the time she returned, Zane had Liam strapped into his car seat, the minivan snug and warm. Her son had Zane's little finger clasped tight in his little fist and was staring up at him adoringly, as Zane sat next to him in the back seat and sang "Santa Claus Is Coming To Town" in a soft mellow baritone.

She opened the driver side and stuck her head in. "Hey, thanks for doing this."

Reluctantly, he disentangled his hand from Liam's, and stepped out of the rear passenger seat. "Glad to help out." He waited as she climbed behind the wheel. "Mr. Pierce okay?"

"He is." Loving the way she could always count on Zane to help out, whenever he was needed, she asked, "So, did you still want to do dinner?" After that false alarm, and the even-longer day, she could use the company.

He looked over at her, as protective as ever. "As long as you let me provide it."

Nora exhaled. Sometimes it was good to be taken care of. Especially by an incredibly kind and sexy man. And it was Christmas, after all.

The season for giving. And taking. And giving...

"You're not going to get any argument there."

His gaze swept over her, lingering briefly on her lips before returning to her eyes. "Meet you in an hour, then?"

"Sounds good." *Really good*, she thought, as another spiral of heat swept through her.

Attempting to keep her mind on the mundane, instead of the sizzling chemistry between them, she asked, "What are we having?"

He flashed a mysterious smile. "That, Nurse Nora, is a surprise."

NORA HAD JUST gotten Liam to sleep and into bed for the night when the doorbell rang. She walked back downstairs.

Wishing she'd had time to change, spruce up her hair. Something. But then that would have made it feel like a date, and it wasn't a date. It was just dinner between two old friends.

She opened the door.

Zane strode in, dressed as he had been before, in a crew neck sweater and jeans, a large take-out bag from the Dairy Barn in his arms. She gazed at him, refusing to be taken in by the blatant desire in his gaze. "You didn't..."

His grin widened. "Our favorite craving when we were overseas."

She set the bag on the dining room table and pulled out the various containers with all the delighted surprise of a kid on Christmas morning. "Chili dogs, root beer and onion rings."

"And dark-chocolate peppermint ice cream!"

Wow.

"I gather you're pleased?"

Was this what it would be like to be taken care of by him, all the time? "Very."

Her heart fluttering in her chest, she stashed the ice cream in the freezer and got out the plates and utensils. He looked so darn good here.

So right.

Together, they loaded their plates with hot, fresh food.

"What do you think they put in their chili anyway, that makes it so damned good?" Zane asked, as they began to eat.

Nora shook her head. She was no slouch in the kitchen, thanks to the many lessons her grandmother had given her when she was growing up. Zane was pretty competent, too. But the recipe for this stymied them both.

She savored the spicy, cheesy goodness. The crisp crunch of an onion ring. "No clue." She met his intent gaze and smiled. "All I know is that no matter how we tried to duplicate it when we were deployed overseas we could never really get close. It was always missing something."

He nodded, looking relaxed. Happy. Powerfully masculine... "I remember."

Nora remembered, too. So much. Their happy reunions. The worry she'd had whenever he had been hurt on a mission. The joy they'd experienced when they were together. The heartbreak and loneliness they'd felt when they were apart.

She wasn't sure she could go back to that kind of topsy-turvy life. But the truth was, Zane filled up her heart and her soul the way no one else ever had. Or ever would.

And much as she might want to discount that, she couldn't.

Gratitude for all he'd done for her that day increasing even more, she rose to clear the table. "Thank you. This really hit the spot."

He moved to help her, his gaze moving over her lingeringly, as if he were already mentally ending this evening by making love to her. "What can I say?" he drawled, as he joined her at the sink. "I aim to please."

Her phone rang. The caller ID said Laramie Gardens.

"I'm sorry… I have to take this." She picked it up to answer, but to her dismay, the report was not good. "You're sure you can handle it?" she asked the night supervisor. "Call me if you need my help. Thanks."

"Problem with Mr. Pierce again?" Zane asked when she joined him at the sink.

"No." Nora bent to put their dishes in the dishwasher. "He's fine. Another resident just got news her daughter's family is not going to be able to be with her for Christmas or New Year's this year—they are going to see the son-in-law's parents." She sighed, her heart going out to the wonderful senior citizen. "So she's very upset."

She grabbed two spoons and the container of ice cream from the freezer and headed into the living room.

Zane settled beside her on the sofa. "I guess in that situation you have to take turns."

Nora sat close enough to share, her thigh nudging Zane's. "I think Miss Isabelle would be fine with having them with her every other year." She worked off the lid and offered him first dibs. "But they never spend any of the holidays with her. It's always his folks. And since her husband died last year, they are the only family she has left."

Zane used his own spoon to offer her the first bite. "Not nice."

The decadent treat melted on Nora's tongue. "No," she sighed, offering Zane a taste from her spoon, too. "It's not."

Their eyes met. Held.

Zane fed Nora another bite. "I don't suppose you could interfere?"

Aware they hadn't done this since the last time they were together, Nora did the same.

"No," she said. "Much as I'd like to call Miss Isabelle's

daughter and give her a piece of my mind, I can't. Not that it would do any good." She shrugged unhappily. "From what I've observed in situations like this one, the kindest souls are always the ones who lose out."

Zane regarded her steadily, no more willing to give up on this than he was on the two of them. "Is there anything I can do to help?" he asked softly.

"Well…" Nora paused, smiling as her next idea hit. "Now that you mention it…maybe there is!"

Chapter Seven

"Adopt a grandparent?" Miss Isabelle repeated in consternation late Tuesday afternoon.

While Nora watched, Zane stood in the doorway of the elegant older woman's suite and explained, "I've been tapped to do some kid sitting for my nephew Braden after school today while his parents do some Christmas shopping. I also promised Nora I'd help her get the garlands hung around the community room, so…since Braden likes to draw and color, and you used to teach art at the local high school, I thought maybe you could help us out a little?"

Twin spots of color glowed in the older woman's cheeks. "Just for today," Miss Isabelle clarified anxiously.

"Actually, if it goes well," Nora cut in, "it might become a new volunteer program at Laramie Gardens for anyone who's interested."

"And this is because you two feel sorry for me?" Miss Isabelle asked pertly. "Because I won't have any family with me at Christmas?"

Never one to run from potential conflict, Zane looked Miss Isabelle square in the eye. "I've been in the military ten years. In that time, counting right now, I've only been able to be with my family for four of the Christmas holidays."

And he and Nora had never been together on Christmas Eve or Christmas Day, she thought sadly.

Until this year.

This year held potential.

"So, yeah," Zane admitted candidly, running a thoughtful hand across his jaw, "I know that being separated from loved ones this time of year totally sucks. And in that sense, I'll admit it. I do feel for you."

Miss Isabelle arched an elegant brow in Nora's direction.

"My parents were in the Army and were seldom home for holidays, too," Nora put in with a commiserating glance. "It hasn't gotten much better since I've grown up."

Zane folded his arms in front of his chest and continued, "But we also know that there are a lot of kids who—for a variety of reasons—are in similar straits. So, if we can pair the older with the younger and expand everyone's sense of family and make them all happy, why not?"

Why not indeed? "And if you're willing to be the test case for the proposed program…?" Nora began.

"How old is your nephew?" Miss Isabelle cut in.

Zane smiled fondly and walked over to show Miss Isabella a picture. "Braden just turned six. And though he's lucky enough to have plenty of family, he's also got a six-month-old baby brother…"

Miss Isabelle smiled knowingly. "So in other words, he's now having to *share* the spotlight."

"And though Braden loves Josh a lot, I think he could do with a little special attention."

"But," Nora put in, holding up a palm, lest they get ahead of themselves, "if you don't feel up to it, Miss Isabelle, or choose not to participate at this time, we both understand. We don't want you to feel pressured."

The former art teacher stiffened indignantly. "Of

course I want to meet this adorable young man!" She handed the photo back to Zane. "When did you say he would be here?"

Zane looked at his watch. "Thirty minutes."

Miss Isabelle rose. "Then I better get ready."

Zane and Nora thanked her. Together, they exited the room and walked companionably down the hall, toward her office. "Good job," she told him.

He slid a hand beneath her elbow, then used the leverage to stop her in her tracks and turn her toward him. "It was your idea."

She reveled in their brief moment of privacy. "You sold it."

He leaned down to whisper in her ear. "*We* sold it."

Nora sucked in a breath. "Now, if only all our problems were that easy to solve," she said.

Zane exhaled, the weight of the world suddenly in his eyes. "No kidding," he said.

"YOU TWO MAKE a really good team," Miss Mim complimented Zane and Nora an hour later.

Having promised a group of seniors she would let them all have a turn cuddling Liam, before she left for the day, Nora settled her son in Miss Mim's arms. Zane, who'd been regaling some of the men with his exploits, hovered nearby. He turned, showing none of the worry he had briefly evidenced earlier. With a charming grin, he asked, "In what way?"

Nora could think of lots of ways.

At work.

At home.

In bed.

Betty Blair nodded discreetly in the direction of one

of the craft tables. "You got Miss Isabelle to come out of her suite and smile again."

Nora and Zane turned. Evidently as pleased as she was to see that Miss Isabelle and Braden were still chatting and coloring diligently, Zane lifted a staying hand. "Don't credit me for that. The proposed program had been on Nora's mind for a while now."

"But you made it happen, Lieutenant," Miss Sadie said.

That he had, Nora thought with glowing admiration.

With all she had on her agenda during the holidays, she likely wouldn't have had the time or opportunity to do anything like this until after the New Year.

"Nora, dear," Miss Patricia pleaded, "give the poor fella another chance."

The group of seniors around them nodded, in full matchmaking agreement.

Buck Franklin winked flirtatiously. "If I were another forty years younger, I'd give you a run for your money, soldier."

Nora blushed at all the attention while Zane chuckled. "Good thing you're not, then," he drawled, stepping in to wrap a possessive arm about Nora's waist.

Russell Pierce furrowed his brow. "Does that mean you're still determined to win her back? Because you don't have much time left, if that's the case..."

Twenty-three days, Nora thought. Not that she was keeping track or anything...

With a glance directly into her eyes that telegraphed otherwise, Zane told the group, "We're concentrating on being just friends."

His good-natured assessment was not met with glee. Miss Patricia knitted her hands together. "Then, Nora, *you* do something!"

Exasperated, Nora stepped out of the warm arc of Zane's embrace. "Like what?"

All eyes went to one thing she had yet to notice, prominently placed in the center of the community room.

Mistletoe. Nora flushed at the implication. "Whoa now. I'm working."

Miss Mim gave Miss Sadie a turn with Liam. "Actually," Betty Blair said, keeping track of everything, as per always, "you were off half an hour ago."

"I need to get this done." Nora gestured at the box of stockings, meant for the community room fireplace.

Miss Patricia relieved Nora of the decorations. "It's your own tree that needs trimmed, Nurse Nora."

She huffed. "I put it up." She just hadn't had time to do much else.

Darrell Enlow looked at Zane. "You should be a gentleman and help her with that."

Molly and Chance Lockhart walked in to pick up Braden.

Catching the tail end of the conversation, Zane's sister-in-law agreed. "That's exactly what his brother and I are thinking! Don't let this golden opportunity go by... especially when it comes to a once-in-a-lifetime love."

Nora felt the blood rush to her face. "Who said anything about love?" she couldn't help but blurt out.

Liam was shifted to Miss Patricia. "We all see it, dear."

Zane gave Nora a smug look. "Don't you start!" Nora warned.

He shrugged. "Doesn't seem like I have to."

Disliking the expectant way everyone was looking at them, Nora glowered at the entire group, "Well, you-all are going to have to get over your disappointment because I am *not* going to kiss him."

Zane ambled closer, a devilish look on his face. "Then I'll guess I'll have to kiss you."

Nora gasped, as he bent her backward from the waist. Afraid if he kissed her again, she really would lose herself in this moment—this man—to disastrous result, she spread her hands across his broad chest. "Zane Lockhart," she warned as their eyes met, held, "don't you dare!"

Dark silver eyes shuttering to half-mast, he dared in a low husky voice that further stirred her senses, "Tell me that again five minutes from now, sweetheart, and I'll believe you. Until then…"

He lowered his lips to hers and delivered a kiss to end all kisses. Sweet, tempting. Adoring and tender. Passionate, yet incredibly restrained, too…

It was, Nora realized as she surrendered the way she always inevitably surrendered to Zane, the kind of ultra-romantic kiss that ended a wedding ceremony and began a marriage. The kind of kiss that spoke of the days and weeks and months and years to come. The kind of kiss that forever linked two hearts and souls.

When it finally ended, Zane lifted his head and gazed into her eyes. The silence in the room such that you could have heard a pin drop.

"Tell me," he whispered.

That she didn't want him to kiss her like this? That she didn't want him in her life? Dear Lord… Her knees went weak. She couldn't speak. Couldn't deny him any more than she could deny herself.

With a look of immense satisfaction, he lowered his mouth again. Kissed her even more tenderly. Longing swept through her, and then all was lost in the heart-pounding passion engulfing them both.

Zane hadn't really thought she'd let him kiss her. Not

in front of an audience. But now that she had, the soft press of her body against his, mixed with the sweet give of her lips, was enough to nearly send him over the edge.

Whatever happened next, however, was not destined to happen here. Reluctantly, he lifted his head and ended the soul-shattering kiss. Dimly became aware of the claps, gasps and whistles.

"Hallelujah!" Wilbur Barnes said.

"Finally!" Darrell Enlow chortled.

"About time the two of you came to your senses!" Zane's brother Chance declared.

"I agree about the last," Nora muttered beneath her breath, struggling to regain her balance.

Gallantly, Zane brought her upright. She sent him a withering look, not about to let his actions go unchallenged. "I can't believe you just did that!"

He could. He'd do it again, too.

Taking in Nora's resentment-filled glare, Buck Franklin elbowed him. "You've got your work cut out for you, buddy!"

That was okay. Zane chuckled. He knew he was up to the task.

NORA WASN'T SURPRISED when her doorbell rang at six-thirty that evening. Liam in her arms, she went to answer it. Zane was on her doorstep, a shopping bag in each hand.

Liam grinned up at him.

"Hey, little fella," Zane said, bending down to buss her son's forehead. "I'm happy to see you, too." His amused glance drifted over her. "Can't say your mommy feels the same enthusiasm about my presence, however."

She did and she didn't. And yet time was already passing, too fast… She propped her free hand on her hip and huffed, "Are you here to apologize for kissing me?"

He flashed a grin as wide as Texas. "Never, darlin'! That clinch made my day! Hell, my week! My year, my life…!"

She couldn't help it; she laughed and ushered him inside.

Expression sobering, he crossed the threshold and removed his coat, looping it over the stand next to the front door. Picking up the bags, he carried them over to the sofa table in the living room, so she could see. "I am sorry for embarrassing you in front of everyone. So I brought you and Liam a present, in way of apology."

She peeked inside the bag. "Cool-touch Christmas lights." Excitement zinged through her. There were enough boxes to really light up the unadorned tree in her living room.

Zane mugged at Liam, who was still staring raptly at their visitor. He was then rewarded with a slow smile and an infant gurgle of delight. Zane tucked his little finger inside Liam's tiny fist, as had become their custom. The baby tugged on Zane's hand excitedly.

"Miss Sadie told me the ones your grandparents used to use, years ago, weren't as safe as you'd like."

Enthralled by the bond Zane and Liam had already established, Nora nodded appreciatively. "That's true. Luckily, the ornaments are all still really nice." She pointed to a red storage box next to the tree. "Unfortunately, you can't put the ornaments on until you have the lights on."

Zane turned to survey the task. "I can help with that if you'd like."

Before she had a chance to answer, Liam let go of Zane's finger. Then, surprising them all, he reached for

Zane, grabbing hold of his sweater, and tried to propel himself into the lieutenant's arms. Zane acted fast to catch Liam and hold him against his broad chest.

Nora gasped in wonder. "That's the first time he's ever done that!"

Liam chortled happily and tightly grasped Zane's cashmere sweater. The big guy grinned. "Finally, I'm in the right place at the right time," he boasted.

"Apparently." Had the two ever looked more like father and son than at that moment, their eyes sparkling happily, blond heads together? Nora didn't think so.

Zane cuddled Liam closer. "He's never done that for you?"

"No," she admitted, a little hurt.

"I'm sure it's just because he doesn't have to hurl himself into your arms. You always take him immediately and hold him when you see him after the two of you have been apart."

That was true, Nora admitted. It did not however in any way diminish the special relationship Liam and Zane were forming.

Zane handed Liam back to Nora, but Liam immediately reached for him again. When Zane hesitated, Liam let out a rebel yell.

Amused by her son's strong will, Nora smiled, suggesting, "How about you hold him for a while, and I'll unspool some of the lights?"

Zane sat down with Liam in the rocking chair and turned the baby so he could see his mom, too. Swayed him gently while she draped lights from the bottom of the tree, upward. She had just reached the middle of the tree when she noted Liam was fast asleep.

"We really should put him down in his crib upstairs," she said. "It's his bedtime."

"We?" Zane whispered, looking slightly alarmed by the prospect.

Nora ambled closer, unable to help but note once again how sweet the two men in her life looked. "Well, you're holding him," she whispered back. "And the less we transfer him around, the less likely he is to wake up."

Zane straightened cautiously. "Only one problem," he quipped, as the two moved smoothly toward the stairs. "I don't really know how to do that."

Nora curved a hand around the swell of his bicep. "I'll teach you."

Together, they went upstairs into the softly lit nursery. Nora put the side of the crib down.

"Okay," she directed in a hushed voice, "put one hand behind his head, use the other to support his spine. Then slowly lower him down to the mattress. Set him down, wait a minute, then ease your hands out from under him."

As Zane finished, Liam sighed drowsily.

Nora took Zane's big hand in hers and placed it gently over Liam's chest until they were sure that Liam was fast asleep once again, then carefully withdrew their touch. Ever so quietly, Nora eased the safety rail up and clicked it back into place.

She turned on the monitor. Taking Zane's hand again, she nodded to the door and they quietly exited the room.

"You make it all look so easy," he complimented her when they reached the first floor once again.

Nora thought of the way she had struggled to make everything work when she'd first brought Liam home from the hospital. And then, several weeks after that, home to Texas. How different things would have been if only she'd had Zane here to share that time with her. "Ha!"

He put his hands on her shoulders. "I'm serious."

She knew that. It's what made their situation all the more poignant and intense.

"You really seem to know what you're doing. From what I understand, that's not always the case."

Nora led the way back to the tree. She picked up the strand of lights where she'd left off. Zane grabbed the other end. "Well…all nursing students do rotations in maternity and pediatrics. So I learned how to handle babies there."

"But…?" They moved in tandem around the tree.

Finished with one, they added another strand and began decorating the top half of the tree. "Being a mom, 24-7, is a lot more demanding. There's so much you have to learn. Luckily, most of the women at Laramie Gardens have cared for infants, so I've gotten a lot of helpful tips. Plus, assistance holding and rocking him during what is otherwise his fussiest time of the day."

"Early evening."

"Mmm, hmm."

Her cell phone rang. Nora looked at the caller ID. "It's Davina."

"Want me to step outside?"

Nora shook her head, already answering. "Hey, sis. Still in Qatar?"

"Roger that," Davina retorted happily. "Although I may be moving back to AFRICOM in Stuttgart, Germany, soon." Davina went on to tell Nora a little bit about her latest assignment, which sounded both challenging and exciting…

When it was her turn to talk, Nora said, "I just put Liam down, but if you want to FaceTime so you can see how big he's getting, I'll wake him…"

"No, don't do that." Davina's response was adamant.

"Or I could just take the phone up there, and let you

see him sleeping?" Nora hated the desperation in her voice.

The ever-present need for a familial connection that never really seemed to come.

"Just send me a photo when you have time," Davina went on briskly. "Listen, I got your note about Liam's Christmas gift. You can get him anything you want from me. Just put my name on it. And send me the bill. And you may want to do the same for Mom. You know how bad The General is about remembering stuff like that."

Really bad, Nora acknowledged miserably.

Still, she tried again. "You sure you don't want to at least help pick out the gift? I could send you a few choices."

"I don't have time," her sister retorted, "and anyway, I'm sure you know best. Got to go. I'll call again soon. Okay? And if I don't talk to you before then, merry Christmas!"

Nora choked out, "Merry Christmas to you, too." Doing her best not to cry, she cut the connection.

"Everything okay?" Zane asked, as Nora put her cell phone back on the charger. Briefly, she explained.

"You were hoping for a different outcome," Zane guessed sympathetically.

Nora nodded, as tears began to fall.

The next thing she knew, Zane's arms were around her. He held her close while the storm inside her raged.

He stroked a hand through her hair. "Davina's disinterest doesn't have anything to do with Liam," he said.

"I know that." Nora sniffed.

He pressed a kiss to the top of her head. "Then what's gotten you so upset, darlin'?"

She'd held her worry inside for way too long. She had to confide in someone. Nora swallowed around the ache in her throat. "What's going to happen to Liam if anything ever happens to me?" She drew back to look into Zane's eyes. "Is my little boy going to end up like Miss Isabelle? Deserted by those who should love him and be there for him, but just won't...for whatever reason?" Selfish reasons.

Zane carefully wiped away her tears with the pads of his thumbs. Briefly, he looked as miserable as she felt. "I'd like to say no, but..." His voice trailed off. He searched her face for a long moment, then frowned in concern. "You don't have a guardian lined up?"

Guilt rolled through her with the force of a tsunami. Reluctantly, she shook her head. "I know I should. The lawyer who handled the adoption advised me to get one, but...no. I don't."

"Then how about me?"

Chapter Eight

Nora stared at Zane in amazement. "You want to be Liam's backup guardian?"

Actually, he wanted to be the little fella's daddy, but afraid that he'd scare Nora off again, he said, instead, "Yes. Especially if it will help give you peace of mind."

Her sky blue eyes narrowed in consternation. "But if you're not here, then…"

He had already told Nora he was not reenlisting. Obviously, she did not believe him. No one who knew him did. Figuring she'd realize how serious he was when his actions bore out his promise, he reminded her, "I was prepared to step up and take paternal responsibility for him—when I came back."

"Yes!" She threw up her arms and began to pace the length of her cozy living room. "Yes. When you thought Liam was your child."

He tore his eyes from the flattering red corduroy shirt and jeans she'd put on after work. The shirt buttoned all the way down the front, curved in at the waist and hugged her body in all the right places, just like her dark denim jeans.

"He still could be."

Pretty cheeks flushed, she spun back around to face him.

She took a step closer, looking more beautiful and impassioned than ever before. "In a worst-case scenario."

The doubt in her voice made him want to reassure her.

"And best case, too." He flashed a grin, but his heart lurched when she just stared blankly at him. "Unless you can see someone else as his daddy?" Zane pressed.

"Whoa now, soldier." Hands up in surrender, Nora took a deep breath and backed away. "Now we're really getting ahead of ourselves."

Not in his view. He wanted her to be able to count on him. The way she'd never been able to count on anyone else.

"Not necessarily," he reiterated gruffly, closing the distance between them and taking her hand in his. "I've always felt connected to you, Nora. From the time we were kids and spent summers hanging out together." They'd had something special from that first moment. A shimmer of awareness. An undeniable bond. It was still there. Would always be—if he had anything to do with it.

She gazed down at their entwined hands. Let out a quavering breath. "I've always felt connected to you, too," she confessed softly.

Seeing a chink in her emotional armor, he pointed out, "Our dual stints in the military only intensified that."

She disengaged their palms and moved away. Her eyes locked on his. "Except now I'm out, Zane. For good."

And he still had to go back. For a few weeks, anyway.

Refusing to let that be a roadblock, he moved closer. Continued resolutely, "I was prepared to leave the service for Liam as soon as I heard about him. I'm *still* ready to do that."

Nora looked at him as if none of what he said computed. Peering down at her, he took in the tousled state of her hair and her flushed cheeks. "You need to know that Liam will always be taken care of. That he'll have family and be loved, whether you're here or not," Zane said practically. "You need to know that there will be a rock-solid backup plan for him." Without warning, his voice grew unaccountably rusty. "I want that for the little guy, too."

Nora's lower lip quavered.

Her vulnerability broke his heart. Resolutely, he continued, promising firmly, "If you let me step up here, you'd never have to worry that Liam would end up alone or be forgotten."

Nora stared up at him, thinking, considering.

Zane paused to let his words sink in. "No matter what, he'd have the *whole Lockhart clan* there for him. My four sibs, their spouses, my mom…"

"That's quite an offer," she said, her voice abruptly turning rusty, too.

And one that came straight from his heart. He studied the soft shimmer in her eyes. "The question is," he rasped, inhaling the sweet lavender scent of her, "will you take me up on it?"

NORA DIDN'T KNOW what to say to that.

She knew what she wanted to say, of course. Yes, yes, jingle bells all the way, yes! But if this was a pity ploy…

She folded her arms tightly in front of her. Challenged him emotionally, "It all depends. Are you doing this out of some misplaced sense of duty or honor?"

He stepped close, his brow furrowed. "Because I'm not Liam's biological daddy but could have been?"

He radiated pure masculine strength and his nearness made her want to kiss him again. Nora swallowed around the parched feeling in her throat. "Because of the way things ended between us the last time we called a halt to whatever-this-has-always-been," she said with difficulty, staring into his eyes. "Because you made promises to me before. About quitting…"

"That I ended up not keeping," he interjected grimly.

"Yes."

"I hadn't thought about it that way. But I do want to make it up to you, for all the things I've done backward or badly in the past."

Nora sighed and shook her head. "You don't have to do that. I was at fault, too. I wanted to keep both feet out the door every bit as much as you did."

"True." Crinkles appeared at the corners of his eyes. "But I could have been more traditional about it from the first. Made sure that you felt like the fine Texas lady you are."

She knew what he was getting at, but she had never felt used. The two of them had both gone into their tempestuous affair with their eyes wide-open. They'd both known what they were risking and chosen to take the leap anyway.

She went back to decorating the tree. "I'm an independent woman, Zane. Always have been. Always will be."

He followed and began to help. "An independent woman who still needs a backup plan for Liam." Their fingers brushed as they draped the end of the light strand near the top of the tree. "Because you know the way life is." They stepped back, to view the gorgeously lit tree.

Zane caught her hand, clasped it warmly in his. "If you have insurance of any kind, you'll likely never need it." He shook his head. "The minute you don't…"

Nora sighed as she pivoted to face him. "You find yourself in one heck of a mess."

"Right." Zane wrapped his arms around her. Gently, he smoothed the hair away from her cheek. "So think of my stepping in as a way of guaranteeing that Liam's future—and yours—is every bit as happy and wonderful as it deserves to be."

Nora splayed her hands across Zane's chest. Beneath her fingertips, she felt the steady thrumming of his heart.

She wasn't surprised he was protecting her.

He was always rushing to rescue someone.

It was in his nature.

"This won't change anything between us." It wouldn't make him fall in love with her, in the boundless way she wanted to be loved. "This agreement won't change who and what we are."

His eyes darkened. "I know that."

She studied his sober expression. "You don't care?" Because a part of her did. Very much!

A corner of his mouth quirked up. "I wouldn't say that," Zane drawled in the sexy timbre she loved.

He lowered his head. Kissed her lightly. And his eyes smoldered all the more. "I wouldn't say that at all."

He deepened the kiss, and need swept through her. Taking his head in her hands, she rose on tiptoe, and then with an aggression she had never let herself unleash before, she pressed herself against him and poured every bit of passion and longing she had into the steamy embrace.

Zane groaned, his unbridled hunger coming through loud and clear. The years of wanting and needing, coming together only to separate again, accumulated into a soaring, desperate yearning.

"I want you," he muttered.

Nora gazed breathlessly up at him. "I want you, too."

Taking him by the hand, she led him upstairs, to her bedroom. Instead of heading for the bed, she backed him up against the wall. And then all was lost in the thrilling press of mouths and bodies.

He kissed her like he'd never get enough of her. She kissed him back in exactly the same way, sliding her hands beneath the hem of his sweater, moving her palms up and over the width of his shoulders and the satiny smooth muscles of his back.

She kissed his neck, his jaw, each corner of his lips. Felt him shudder in response.

Lower still, there was a tsunami of desire. Pressing against the front of his jeans. Dampening hers...

The next thing she knew, her shirt and bra were coming off. Their positions were reversed. It was her back against the wall, and his sweater was coming off. They came together once again, her breasts nestled in the soft mat of hair sprinkled across his chest, her breath catching.

He bent his head, ravishing her lips again, using the flat of his palms, then the pads of his thumbs to tease her nipples into aching crowns. When she could stand it no more, his touch drifted lower still, unfastening her jeans, sliding inside the satin of her panties. Finding her there. His fingers exploring the slick folds, sliding inside her. Making lazy forays. Moving in and out and in again.

"I thought I was supposed to be in charge here," Nora gasped.

"In due time..."

He drove her crazy with his touch, making her feel more womanly and wanton than she ever had in her entire life. Until her body ignited and she was so consumed with wanting him inside her she could barely breathe.

Needing to give as well as receive, she tried to wrestle free. He held fast. Lowering, delivering the most intimate of kisses. Thrilling, she slipped right over the edge, into ecstasy.

When the delicious shudders had finally ceased, she

kicked completely free of her jeans. Divested him of his. And then, her heart brimming with feeling, knelt to show him just how talented she could be. Flush with victory, she discovered the hardness of his body, the fierceness of his desire. Sending him right to the brink.

He lifted her up. She rolled on his condom and he possessed her with one smooth stroke. Awash with sensation, she clamped her legs around his waist and rose up to meet him. He lifted her, going deeper, slower, stronger. Bringing them closer, making them one. And then there was nothing but the hot, melting bliss.

The two of them clung together for long moments. Knees weak. Hearts pounding.

"About this," Zane said finally. "About us…"

Nora had no idea what he was going to say. His expression was so inscrutable.

She knew what she wanted, however.

"How about we take it one day at a time?" she suggested recklessly. "Just…" She inhaled a quavering breath. "Let what happens…happen…"

For a moment, she thought he was going to ask for something else. What, she wasn't exactly sure.

Then, to her immense relief, he smiled and nodded. Threading his hands through her hair, he lowered his head and delivered another soul-stirring kiss. "Sounds good to me," he muttered gruffly, inciting her passion all over again. "And what I'd like now…" He lifted her in his arms and carried her to her bed. Following her down, he stretched out beside her. "Is this…"

And "this," as it turned out, was more than good enough for her. More than good enough for both of them.

Two days later, Zane sat at his dining room table, surrounded by mounds of paper. Résumé, credit report, income tax returns. Financial and bank statements. A half-finished business plan and lists of assets still needing to be purchased, facilities built.

Hearing a car in the lane, he put the lengthy application he was working on aside. Groaned at what he saw.

Not about to let his mom see what he was currently working on, he grabbed his jacket, the big box of outdoor holiday decorations and the toolbox she'd brought over to him the previous weekend. "Hey, Mom. Great timing. Want to help me put up the lights?"

Lucille made her way up the walk, looking elegant as ever in a designer wool coat, scarf and heels.

"Ah... Not really."

Zane held out a cushioned deck chair for her. "You can sit and keep me company then."

Lucille looked longingly toward the inside of his ranch house. "It's a little chilly out here."

"Hang on." Zane dashed inside and returned carrying a velvety lap blanket with a shearling underside. "So what brings you out here?"

Lucille pulled a pair of fine leather gloves from her pocket and inched them on. "I wanted to know if it was true. Have you been making the rounds to the West Texas Warriors Assistance, the sheriff, fire and EMS departments, as well as the local airstrip, talking about employment?"

Not about to jinx anything at such a precarious stage, Zane pounded a few nails in, above the windows. "Just checking out my options, Mom. I'll have to do something when I do get out of the military."

Lucille paused, the way she always did when she was about to jump ahead to what was really on her mind.

"Is the misunderstanding about Liam's paternity the

only thing that brought you back to Laramie for the holidays?"

Zane moved the ladder a little farther down. "No." He had already planned to return to Laramie when he was on leave, because he knew Nora had settled here. He had wanted to see if they could somehow make a go of it again. Not wanting to get into all that with his mother, however, he resumed hammering and said, "I also wanted to see you and the rest of the family."

Lucille tucked the blanket more closely around her. "Is Liam the only reason you were even considering not reenlisting in January?"

Initially. Zane strung snowflake lights across the windows, above the doors, then moved his ladder to the other side. "If he had been my biological son, it would have been the right thing to do."

"And now that you know he's not your child?"

For a whole host of other reasons, it was still the right thing to do.

He squinted at his mother. "I don't appreciate the inquisition, Mom."

Lucille turned up the collar on her coat. "If I didn't pry just a little, I would never know anything about your life."

True, but there were some things she didn't need to know about. Zane regarded his mother steadily. He knew he was the baby of the family, but she had to let him grow up sometime. "Maybe we should change the topic," he suggested.

She watched as he resumed his hammering. "Fine. We'll talk about all the time you've been spending at Laramie Gardens, then. I hear you're quite popular around there."

Grinning, Zane moved his ladder down the porch again. "I like it there. Reminds me of the summers I spent with Grandpa, when I was a kid. Plus I knew a fair number of the residents, like Mr. Pierce, the former owner of the Book Nook, and Miss Mim, the town librarian back then, too."

His mother smiled. "So you're fond of them."

Zane nodded. He went back to stringing snowflake lights. "Their various life experiences give them a valuable take on the world. They're constantly reminding me that life is short. You've got to grab it with both hands while you can."

"I thought that's what you've been doing with the Special Forces."

Zane knew his mom hated what she saw as his way-too-dangerous-occupation. "It is." But Nora and Liam had been teaching him there was more to life than just protecting and serving their country, too.

"Is that what you are also back to doing with Liam's mother, Nora Caldwell? Living in the moment? Grabbing life with both hands?"

Briefly, Zane dropped his head. "What happened to the ultradiscreet mother I used to have?"

Lucille got up and walked over to him. "She vanished in the wake of the Lockhart Foundation scandal that rocked Dallas a few years ago."

Zane knew that was true. His mother had gone from trusting too much to challenging everything.

She looked him in the eye. "I'm going to be direct with you, son. You have to quit treating your never-ending love affair with Nora Caldwell like it's some dirty little secret!"

Wow. Talk about a shot right to the heart. "Mom! Seriously!"

Lucille held her ground. "Laramie is a small town. Where everyone knows everyone else, and watches out for everyone else. When your pickup truck is parked in front of her house every night, sometimes all night, like it has been the last few evenings, people notice. Even when the two of you keep declaring to one and all that the two of you are not officially dating."

Zane had never liked being backed into a corner. He liked it even less now.

"It's none of their business, Mom." Although he'd made it clear to the matchmaking residents of Laramie Gardens that Nora had won him over long ago.

"Maybe not, but everyone sees the sparks between the two of you. They have for years now."

Zane exhaled roughly. "So?"

"So the two of you are both thirty years old. Why have you never gotten married or even engaged? Why do the two of you keep pretending to others there is nothing much between you?"

Because Nora had always wanted it that way. And when it came to public perception of them, he chose to honor her wishes. "It's complicated."

Lucille waited.

"When we were teenagers there really was nothing to report. We were just very good friends." Who secretly lusted after each other, yet feared doing anything that would potentially impact their friendship.

Lucille's expression gentled. "And when you were in college?"

Zane went back to stringing lights. "We were thousands of miles apart. Our contact was limited to email, phone, text messaging." Although they'd both burned up the wires doing that.

Lucille watched him retrieve an additional strand. "And once you each graduated and went on active duty?"

Reality and fantasy, want and need, had all begun to blend. "With her in the armed services, too," Zane reflected, "our relationship became even more complicated."

Lucille followed, her high heels tapping across the deck. "Because?"

Zane paused to remove the new strand from the packaging. "There are military regulations, Mom. Fraternization, especially between nurses and their patients, is frowned upon."

"She only cared for you personally once, that time you injured your shoulder on a mission and had to have surgery in Germany."

"Yes, but I've been in and out of the military hospitals where she's been on the nursing staff multiple times."

"With gunshot and shrapnel wounds," Lucille recalled with an unhappy shudder. "That one horrible concussion…"

"It wouldn't have been appropriate for Nora to care for me." Because she had been too emotionally involved with him. And he with her.

"Mmm, hmm."

The innuendo in his mother's low tone prompted him to rush to say, "Plus, Brigadier General Caldwell wouldn't have approved if it had been anything more."

The General had wanted Nora to have only one love—the upward trajectory of her career in the Army. Hence, they'd kept their increasingly intimate on-again, off-again relationship as private as possible.

"And you know this how?" Lucille demanded.

Zane looked his mother in the eye. "The same way I know you don't approve of what is or is not going on with me and Nora right now."

"First of all, you don't know what I approve of or not because we haven't discussed it. But, you're right. I am upset to hear via the WTWA grapevine that you're thinking about becoming Liam's guardian, when your relationship with Nora is still so…casual."

"*Backup* guardian, Mom," Zane corrected. "The person who steps in, in the event of an emergency or life-altering circumstance." Which was why he'd had to go over to the West Texas Warrior Assistance and get information on military benefits for active and separated military. Find out what, if anything, Liam would be eligible for. Answer? The way things stood? Not much. Not that he intended to leave it at that, in any case. "We signed the papers at Nora's attorney's office this morning. So it's already official."

"I'm guessing you volunteered for this."

Well, he certainly hadn't been drafted. "Yes."

"Why?"

His mother's near-constant disapproval rankled. "Because Nora needs me. And so does her son."

"If you were seriously dating…or even engaged," his mother continued, frowning, "it might make sense—"

"It makes sense *now*, Mom," he interjected. "Nora doesn't have anyone else to call upon to be there for her son."

"What about her mother and her sister?"

He scrubbed a hand across his face, his patience wearing thin. "Davina isn't the least bit interested in kids. She's all about her career. As far as her mother, The General wasn't there for Nora when she was a kid, and she still isn't."

"Are you?" Lucille asked emphatically.

I'm sure as hell trying to be. As much as she'll let me. Aware his mother was still watching him carefully, he said, "Liam is special."

"I agree."

He wondered at the reason behind her disapproval.

Usually, his mother was all out when it came to helping others. It was why she and his late father had poured most of their fortune into a charitable foundation. "But...?" Zane prodded.

"It's fine to promise Nora all this now, when you are home on leave. But once you're deployed again, you won't be available to either her or her son."

Except he *wasn't* reenlisting. Knowing his mother wouldn't believe it any more than Nora or his siblings did, however, he merely said, "We'll make it work, Mom. Now, and in the future. That's the good thing about both Nora and I. We can adapt."

Something akin to respect glimmered in his mother's eyes. "I can see you're determined," she said finally.

"I am."

"Then behave the way you were brought up," she urged kindly but firmly. "Treat them like the family they are to you. And bring them to dinner at my ranch with the rest of your siblings and their loved ones."

And get even more of the third degree? Zane went back to hanging decorations. "Nora's pretty busy right now."

His mother retrieved her car keys from her purse. "I'm sure she can find time before Christmas. I'll send you a couple of options. If those dates don't work, tell me which one will. Or we could both call her right now..."

As if on cue, Zane's phone went off. It was Nora. Texting SOS—the private code they had used when they were kids. She hadn't used it in years. And she had never once used it lightly.

"Thanks for stopping by, Mom, but I've got to go." Zane escorted Lucille to her car, then rushed off.

Chapter Nine

Twenty minutes later, Zane strode into Laramie Gardens. Nora met him at the door of her office. "What's up?" he asked. Definitely something. The normally unflappable woman he adored looked harried and upset.

She stepped closer and he caught the scent of her lavender perfume. "Mr. Pierce wants you there for his meeting with Dr. Wheeler, the geriatric specialist in charge of his case. Is that going to be okay with you?"

Zane paused. "Instead of his daughter?" Who could probably be available by conference call or Skype?

Her delicate hand lightly cupping his elbow, Nora led him down the hall. "Mr. Pierce will explain his reasoning. But if you're okay with this, I'll have him sign the necessary privacy forms that will allow you to be informed of his medical issues."

"Sure."

Zane followed Nora into the conference room. Russell Pierce was sitting across the table from Ron Wheeler, a genial-looking young man not long out of medical school. The two seemed to be in some sort of standoff.

Zane shook the hands of both men while Nora presented the necessary HIPAA forms to Mr. Pierce, who signed with a shaky hand.

"Thanks for coming, Zane," the dapper older man

said, as Zane took the seat next to him. "I need someone I can trust to put their emotion aside and help me decide what's right."

Zane nodded his assent. "So what's the issue?"

Mr. Pierce pointed at the doctor and nurse on the opposite side of the table. "They want to have hospital tests run on me…"

"MRI, EEG, CT," Dr. Wheeler said.

"It's all outpatient," Nora explained, "and could be done over a couple of days."

Although time-consuming, none of the tests were painful or invasive. Zane leaned forward intently. "So what's the issue?"

Mr. Pierce grimaced. "Say I am in the early stages of a brain tumor or a degenerative disease like Alzheimer's. At eighty-five, I'm too old and frail to have major surgery. And it's my understanding the medicines they have for a lot of the more debilitative neurological conditions don't really work all that well. Bottom line, if there is something really wrong with me, I'm not sure I want to know. Especially at Christmastime."

Zane met his glance equably. "I can understand that," he said. He turned back to Nora, and Dr. Wheeler, lifting a brow in silent inquiry.

"It's true—we could get bad news from the tests," Dr. Wheeler acknowledged. "But we could also get information that would allow us to properly diagnose the reason behind this confusion and disorientation you're now having most evenings."

"Is that guaranteed?" Mr. Pierce persisted.

"No," Dr. Wheeler reluctantly admitted.

"But it's better than doing nothing, while your symptoms slowly but steadily worsen," Nora put in.

Mr. Pierce looked at Zane.

He had to ask. "Does your daughter, Lynn, know about any of this?" From what he had observed, she was very caring.

"No," Mr. Pierce replied stubbornly. "And I don't want Lynn to be informed right now because she'd put me on a plane back to New York City and have all sorts of doctors doing every test imaginable on me. And I don't want that. I want to stay here in Texas. Where my home and heart and late wife and friends all are."

That made sense, too, Zane noted.

"So if I were your parent," Mr. Pierce persisted, looking straight at Zane, "what would you want me to do?"

He returned the older gentleman's straightforward look. "I'd want you to find out the truth behind your condition, if you could, via any test that is not too invasive or uncomfortable for you," he advised kindly.

"And then…?"

Zane continued, "Weigh your treatment options against any probability of success. And then concentrate on the quality of life. Because at the end of the day," he asserted firmly, meeting everyone's eyes, "if you're not really present every minute of every day, then you're not really living."

GRATEFUL FOR ZANE'S COMPASSIONATE, steady presence, Nora walked Zane out to the front of the building. The cold, crisp winter air was a welcome respite from the sometimes stifling heat of the seniors' living facility.

Aware they were being watched by many of their matchmakers, she paused beneath the portico. Keeping a respectful distance from Zane, said, "Thanks for helping out today and volunteering to accompany Mr. Pierce when he goes to the hospital the next couple of days. We could have sent a staff member, but I think he feels more protected, knowing you're going to be there."

Noticing she was beginning to shiver, Zane removed his fleece jacket and draped it over her shoulders.

The warmth of his body, and his woodsy scent enveloped her as surely as one of his hugs. His glance cut to the ladies swooning behind the glass windows of the community room. He shook his head at the lack of privacy, then returned his attention to her face. "Because I'm part of the Special Forces?"

"No," Nora replied, forcing a smile. "Because you're you." Suddenly, inexplicably on the verge of tears, she jerked in a bolstering breath and worked to cover the building emotion within her. Try as she might, the worry over what she was going to do, how she was going to cope when Zane left again in a few weeks was always at the back of her mind.

She whisked an imaginary piece of lint from the hem of her uniform top, teased with a blatant wink. "But you're right, there is something prestigious about taking you anywhere."

He chuckled and shoved his hands in the pockets of his jeans. "Nice to know, sweetheart."

Nora ignored the men now standing at the windows, eating popcorn. It was all she could do not to blush. "Listen. I kind of feel I owe you for this afternoon." She dared almost asking him for a date. "So if you want to come over for dinner later…"

Zane hesitated. "I'd love to," he admitted, his glance drifting affectionately over her face, "but I've got some stuff back at the ranch I have to take care of this evening. Particularly if I'm going to be going to the hospital with Mr. Pierce the next three days."

Doing her best to hide the hurt of rejection, Nora nodded. "Of course."

Had she asked too much? Put too much domestic pressure on Zane? Hard to tell from the suddenly inscrutable expression on his handsome face. Had she somehow made him feel hemmed in, or forced too much upon him, asking him to sit in a hospital for hours on end, cooling his heels when he could be out protecting their country and/or saving the world?

He reached out and gently took her hand. "But there is something you could do for me in return."

"Anything," she said, swallowing hard.

"My mother's having a family dinner on Sunday afternoon. She'd like us both to be there. And of course, she wants you to bring Liam, too."

Stepping back out of view of their cheering section, Nora held Zane's gaze. "What would you like?"

Understanding precisely what she was doing, he moved with her. "To not be put under the familial microscope?"

Nora laughed, as she knew he meant her to.

Guaranteed a few seconds of privacy, he brushed the hair from her temple. "Seriously, I know we promised we'd keep it casual and take it day by day while I'm on leave." A coaxing smile lifted the corners of his sensual lips. "But I'd really like it if you would be my plus one. And Liam my plus two since he is now sort of a member of the Lockhart clan."

The thought of having family standing by for them warmed Nora as much as his jacket. Enthusiasm building, she asked, "What time?"

"I'll pick you up at four. And Nora—" he hugged her briefly and trailed his lips across her cheek "—thanks for this."

ZANE WASN'T SURPRISED Nora and Liam both received a warm welcome at the Circle H Ranch that weekend. Although his family had once been as disconnected as Nora's, his father's illness and death, coupled with a scandal at the family's charitable foundation, had not only made them work as a team, but forged close and loving bonds.

Now, with all four of his siblings married to the loves of their lives and raising families of their own, the pressure was on him to do the same.

Hence, they barely had their coats off before the subject of his romantic future came up. "I can see why you wanted to be this little guy's guardian," his brother Chance remarked, watching as Nora shifted her son to Zane so she could refrigerate the bottles of formula she'd brought.

"Backup guardian," Zane corrected, lounging against the counter, Liam cradled snugly in his arms.

Wyatt and Adelaide grinned at the way Liam was clinging to Zane's collar and cooing adoringly up at him. Each was holding one of their twin toddlers, and they shifted slightly so Nora could take her place beside Zane. "Doesn't look like Liam is differentiating," Wyatt observed.

Unable to help himself, Zane grinned back down at his tiny charge. Darned if the little guy didn't feel like his son. Nora, the woman he was meant to spend the rest of his life with…

Garrett and Hope sauntered over to greet Liam, too, their arms full of their own two boys, almost-two-year-old Max and his newborn brother, Jack. "He definitely seems to know when he's got it good," Garrett observed with the gravity of their oldest sibling, as well as the first among them to actually settle down.

I'm the one who has it good, Zane thought to himself,

aware for the first time he didn't have to envy his siblings' happiness.

Sage pushed her way in to offer their three-month-old guest a cloth covered candy-cane-shaped baby rattle, while Nick followed with their six-month-old son, Shane. "I agree. Nora's little boy is absolutely darling!" She mugged at the infant until Liam mugged back, then tucked her index finger into his tiny fist, declaring, "If anyone can bring Zane back to Texas for good, it's this little fella."

"And his mommy," Lucille added, beaming with enthusiasm.

Zane felt Nora stiffen almost imperceptibly beside him.

Lest she feel pushed into something she wasn't ready for, Zane lifted a staying hand. "Okay, everybody, let's not get ahead of ourselves here."

Nora relaxed, ever so slightly, her shoulder brushing his arm.

Ever the romantic, Sage palmed her chest innocently, and said, "Hey, calm down, bro. We're just saying you-all make a cute family."

Nick elbowed his wife, letting her know with a glance she needed to back off a bit, lest she jinx it. "In the loosest, most casual definition of the word," he clarified.

Although she was still smiling dutifully, Zane knew Nora couldn't be happy about the direction the conversation was taking. At this rate, his family would have them hitched, Liam adopted by him, too, and Nora pregnant in no time.

And although *he* might be ready for all that, Nora had given no sign that *she* was. "I thought we were going to make Christmas cookies for the residents of Laramie Gardens this evening."

Braden piped up. "I promised Miss Isabelle I'd bring her some when I went over to color pictures with her again."

To Zane's relief, his mother got the hint. "Then we better get started," Lucille said.

"You've got to take it down a notch," Zane told Sage, a few hours later, when they went out to the grill, behind the Circle H bunkhouse.

She adjusted the controls on the state-of-the-art gas grill with the precision of the professional chef that she was. "I'm sorry. I'm excited."

Wishing he hadn't had to go to his older sister for business advice, Zane stood by, large glass dish in hand. "I don't want Mom or Nora to know what I'm doing until it's all ready to go."

"Understood." Sage lifted the plastic wrap, and checked on the marinating skirt steak. "How are things going, by the way?"

A helluva lot slower than expected, Zane thought in frustration. "I still need an appraisal and survey done." Along with a substantial small business loan.

"Did you contact Raquel Morrissey at First National, as I suggested?"

"On my list." *My very long to-do list.*

"Listen, Zane, I love the businesspeople here in Laramie. But for a project the size and scope of what you're trying to do, you need to go back to Dallas. And take advantage of all the connections we had growing up."

Garrett joined them. He carried a second dish. This one contained boneless chicken. "Mom says the crew is getting hungry."

"We're hurrying." Sage placed meat on the grill. She looked at the cooking platform and smacked her forehead. "I forgot the veggies. Can you guys handle this for a second?"

Garrett and Zane shrugged in unison. "Sure."

Hands on her hips, Sage regarded them skeptically. "Don't flip anything until I get back. Just make sure it doesn't burn—by turning down the flame, if necessary."

Zane's phone went off. He checked it, then put it back in his pocket without answering.

"Someone from your unit?" Garrett guessed.

Zane exhaled. The only other person who could understand how hard all this was for him was his eldest brother, who had also spent years in the military, as a physician, before resigning to marry and raise a family with Hope. Casting a glance behind him to make sure they were still out of earshot, Zane nodded. "How did you know?"

Garrett shrugged and turned his attention back to the grill, same as Zane. "I figured you would be under a lot of pressure to reenlist."

No joke. He sipped his beer. "They're offering me everything they can think of."

"Like?"

"Promotion, higher salary. Choice of assignment."

"Yeah, well—" Garrett turned and clinked his own bottle against Zane's "—do us all a *very big favor* and don't mention a word of this to Mom until right after Christmas. She deserves a good holiday." Garrett took a drink and shook his head in silent remonstration. "And if she thinks you're leaving again…"

A throat cleared behind them.

Zane turned, expecting to see his sister. Instead, Nora stood there, a half dozen grilling utensils in one hand, two pot holders in another. Her eyes weren't quite meeting his; her face was a blotchy pink and white.

Stepping forward, she flashed both men the kind of

impersonal grin she gave Laramie Gardens residents when they were being a pain. She thrust the items at him and said, "Sage will be right out."

Giving him no chance to reply, she turned and fled.

"ARE YOU GOING to talk to me?" Zane asked, hours later, as they turned onto the lonely country roads back to Laramie.

Nora kept her eyes on the countryside. "It was a long day, Zane. I'm really wiped out."

He imagined that was so. She'd been acting as if nothing at all were wrong for several hours now. Ignoring all his subtle attempts to get her alone for a private chat while they were still at the Circle H ranch. "Then how about we stop by the No Name?" he asked casually, not about to let her call it a night with this misunderstanding still lingering between them.

Her slender shoulders slumped in defeat. "I—"

He reached across and briefly squeezed her hand before letting it go. He returned both hands to the steering wheel. "It won't take long. I have something to show you." Something he really hoped she liked.

He wrinkled his nose as a very particular odor filled the compartment of his pickup truck. "And from the scent of it, Liam needs a little break, too."

NORA THOUGHT SHE'D been embarrassed before. Having walked in on what was obviously a private conversation between the only two brothers in the Lockhart family who had served in the military. A conversation that had seemed to point the way to Zane reenlisting, as she had always expected he would.

But now...

As the odor emanating from the infant seat in the

back seat worsened, she realized it wasn't just a little excess tummy air. Cringing, she turned to Zane. "You smell that, too?" Nothing like a three-month-old baby to take the romance out of an equation! But maybe that was what they needed—a smelly, soiled diaper to bring them back to earth, fast.

And out of this fantasy world she had been living in…

The fantasy world where Liam had not just an in-case-of-emergency-guardian, but a mommy and a daddy and a big, wonderful, loving extended family to go with it…

Zane cast her a look as Liam, in his car seat, waved his arms and kicked his legs and noisily worked on evacuating the last of his dinner.

"In fact," Zane teased with a laugh, "the way our little buddy is going, I think everyone for ten miles is soon going to smell it. And since there is no place to stop for a diaper change between here and town…especially after dark…"

Nora couldn't help it as her son kept up his antics. She laughed, too. "Okay, okay!" She put up surrendering hands. "You win. Your ranch, it is."

Which, truth be told, was where she wanted to be anyway.

She and Zane hadn't had a moment alone all day. And call her crazy, but she missed having her one-on-one time with him. Desperately.

As they drove up the lane, Nora caught the first sight of the No Name ranch house. The A-frame had been completely outlined with twinkling white snowflake lights, making the ranch house stand out majestically against the moonlit fields surrounding it. Her only lament was the fact her son was a little too young to really enjoy the Christmas sight.

"Oh, Zane." Nora pressed a hand to her heart. "That is absolutely gorgeous!"

Grinning, he got out to help her and Liam out of the minivan. "Goes with the wreath on the door, don't you think?"

Nora grabbed her diaper bag, while Zane lifted Liam and his carrier out of the safety seat base in the rear seat. "Is this why you've been so elusive this week?"

Gallantly, he escorted her up the walk. "What do you mean?" He flashed her a stymied look, then paused to punch in the security code on the pad next to the front door. "We saw each other every day at some point. Always had lunch or dinner together." And on three of the four days found time to make love, too.

Nora pointed out curiously, "But then you came back out here, to work on things." Things he had never exactly explained. But that had kept him awfully distracted and busy.

His broad shoulders emanating as much strength as the rest of him, Zane led the way inside. He hit the switches that turned on the lights across the entire first floor of the A-frame, then nodded at the laptop computer, printer, scanner and stacks of folders on the desk behind the sofa. "I've been getting caught up on a lot of paperwork, too."

It certainly looked like it.

Aware the job of changing Liam was going to be a "roll up your sleeves and try not to breathe in" task, Nora eased out of her coat. She tossed it on the sofa. As merry as the exterior was, it still seemed like a total bachelor pad inside. "No tree?"

He inclined his head in a way that seemed to indicate he didn't plan on messing with that.

His eyes twinkled merrily. "But there is something even better," he promised, "that I'll show you once we take care of the little guy." He unstrapped Liam from his carrier, slid his hands beneath and gently lifted her son out.

Too late realizing that Liam's sleeper was damp with leaking brown liquid that soaked into his shirt.

"Oh, no!" Nora grabbed the closest thing—a roll of paper towels from the kitchen—tore off a half dozen and pressed them against Zane's rib cage to mitigate the damage and keep the moisture from leaking down to his pants.

Seeing what was going on, Zane laughed and shook his head at their tiny charge. "Got me again, fella! Good one!"

Liam gurgled, and now that his little intestines were blissfully empty, relaxed against Zane's broad chest.

Nora took in the smelly, awful disaster. "I am so sorry, Zane!"

"Not to worry," Zane chuckled, unperturbed. "He's just initiating me. Letting the 'new man in your life' know who is really boss in this equation." He bussed the top of Liam's head. The baby cooed contentedly and snuggled closer.

Nora rolled up the sleeves on her shirt. "I'm going to have to put him in a bath." Upstairs, Zane had only a steam shower. Which left few options. "Do you think we could use the kitchen sink? I'll sterilize the whole area after."

"Sure." He gave her a leisurely once-over. "What do you need me to do?"

"Crank up the heat down here and grab a few big fluffy towels." She held out her arms. "But first, let me relieve you of your charge."

"You're going to get this on you, too."

"It's okay. I don't wear anything that's not machine washable these days."

The transfer was made.

By the time Zane returned with the towels, Nora had filled the sink with about six inches of warm water and removed the last remaining clean sleeper, packet of travel wipes and baby wash from her diaper bag.

Zane watched her lay Liam down on the first towel. "I hate to say this, but you're covered, too."

Nora made quick work of unsnapping Liam, getting him out of the soggy, soiled diaper and wiped down cursorily as best she could. "All three of us smell delightful."

Zane stripped off his shirt and undershirt. Luckily, the offending goo hadn't reached his skin. Nora laid Liam in Zane's arms, briefly. "Just give me a second to strip down, too." She took off her fitted corduroy shirt, then noting her camisole was damp, too, took that off. Clad in her bra and black skirt, she reached for Liam and gently lowered him into the waiting water.

He grinned with delight as she washed him down, first with a cloth, and then with the liquid baby soap that Zane warmed between his hands before spreading it over Liam's chest, back, arms and legs.

They rinsed him again with the cloth, then brought him out of the water. All nice and clean and smelling of lavender.

Nora placed her son on another clean towel, then dried him off with a third. By the time he was diapered and dressed, he was yawning mightily.

Nora handed him off to Zane. "If you could just walk him around while I tidy up this mess. And…is it okay if I use your washing machine?"

"Please do!" Zane said, so fervently she laughed.

As they wandered off, with Zane softly singing "Good

King Wenceslas," Nora made short work of starting the laundry and restoring his kitchen to its former immaculate state.

By the time she returned to Zane's side, Liam was cuddled against his chest, fast asleep. He turned to her and smiled. "Ready to see my surprise?"

Chapter Ten

Nora was ready for something, all right.

The close proximity to Zane, coupled with their half-dressed states, had her thinking all kinds of wild things.

With a fast-asleep Liam still snuggled in his arms, Zane led the way up the stairs to the second floor of the A-frame. It was just as she recalled, with one exception. The full-size crib, rocking chair and changing table in one corner. She stared in shock. "You set up a nursery?"

Zane shrugged amiably. "I thought Liam might appreciate a comfortable place to be when he is out here on the ranch."

"It's...amazing." And definitely not the actions of a man who had one foot out the door.

He turned to her, exuding the thoughtfulness she so admired. "If you want, we could let him test it out right now."

"You want to put him down?"

He smiled at her incredulous look. "For the night. If you'd like to stay."

Nora edged closer, trying not to let on what his low, sexy voice did to her. Her heart did *not* melt, her insides did *not* turn to mush just listening to him!

"I don't have any nightclothes." It was one thing to make love on impulse and have him stay on for a few hours, holding her in his arms, and then slip out before dawn. That was simply taking their relationship moment by moment, a feat they had done many times before. But it was something else entirely to plan so deliberately to bring her—and Liam—into his day-to-day life.

He stepped closer still, inundating her with his steady masculine warmth. "You can borrow something of mine to wear." Leaning down, he continued softly, persuasively, "I've got diapers and Liam's formula, too."

Aware how very close she was to falling all the way in love with him, she released a reluctant, admiring sigh. "You really are prepared." *And kind and thoughtful. Capable and commanding...*

"Hopeful, always, when it comes to you, and now Liam. And yeah, darlin'—" he paused, a determined, sexy glint in his eyes "—I am. So what do you say?" he asked huskily, "Want to spend your first night ever at the No Name?"

At the moment, Nora couldn't think of a better Christmas gift to herself. And him. "Yes," she whispered back, knowing no matter what the future held, there would never be a man more perfect for her than Zane.

She tiptoed closer to the crib. Beckoned Zane to follow. Her gaze fell to her contentedly drowsing son. Although she knew firsthand there was no cozier place to be than snuggled against Zane's warm body, she also knew her son would sleep more soundly in a crib. "Let's put—" *our son*, she almost said "—Liam to bed."

Oblivious to her near mistake, Zane lowered Liam slowly to the mattress and eased his hands out beneath him. With her at his side, he kept the other resting ever so slightly on her son's tiny chest until he was sure that Liam was still snoozing.

Contentment flowing between them, they backed away.

Zane took Nora's hand in his. Soundlessly, they moved to the other side of the spacious moonlit loft. "Now what?" he asked, drawing her close.

She caught a whiff of his chest, then her own. She wrinkled her nose comically. "I think," she whispered back, wanting to rid them of the lingering noxious scent, "we should both hit the shower."

He reached behind her to undo the zipper on her skirt. "Together?"

She splayed her hands across his chest and felt his heart thud against her palm, in tandem with hers. She fit her lips to his and kissed him seductively. "It will save water."

It wasn't the first time they had stripped down and climbed into a stall together. But it was by far the most intensely passionate, Nora thought, as they lathered each other from head to toe, and then stood together under the spray to rinse.

"I'm sorry I was ticked off at you earlier." She slid her arms around his back and pressed him intimately against her, inhaling the spicy scent of his soap and the even-sweeter fragrance of his hair and skin.

He kissed her fiercely, evocatively, until they were both groaning for more. He turned her so she was facing the tiles, her hands splayed out in front of her. He pulled her back against him, one hand exploring her breasts, the other moving across her tummy, downward. Her hips rocked restlessly against him as his lips made a thorough tour of the sensitive place behind her ear, the vulnerable slope of her neck.

"Nothing has changed since the last time we talked about my commitment to the military," he murmured, as her soft, pliant body surrendered all the more. "My siblings just don't want me talking about it to my mother."

Her whole body was quivering with sensation when he turned her to face him. Aware she hadn't ever wanted him this desperately, Nora looked up at him. "They think she won't believe you?"

The large glass enclosure filled with steam as the water sluiced down over them. He fit her against him once more. Hardness to softness. All the need she had hoped to see was reflected in his gray eyes, and it set her body on fire.

He cupped her head between his large hands and kissed her languidly at first, then with building ardor, rubbing against her, driving her to the brink. "You didn't."

Her erect nipples ached as she surged against him once more. Going up on tiptoe, she wreathed her arms about his neck. A shuddering sigh escaped her lips. "I'm beginning to."

"Good." He lowered his mouth to hers. Kissed her deeply. Then more and more rapturously.

"Because I want you to know how much I care," he rasped against her mouth, finding her with his fingertips, possessing her, body and soul. Until she felt it, too. In every kiss and caress. Needing and giving. As lovers, as equals, as friends. And maybe even, she thought, as he continued to make sweet love to her, as something even more...

An hour before, Zane hadn't figured the evening would end as he wanted, with the two of them in each other's arms. Never mind in his shower. But as they rolled on a condom and settled onto the teak bench against the wall, Nora straddling his lap, kissing him as if it were an end in and of itself, he knew things were changing.

She was opening herself up to him in a way she never had before. Drawing out the moment. Celebrating the occasion. Taking everything he offered. Possessing him, as well. Until there was nothing in the world but the two of them and this all-encompassing bliss. And he knew if she continued to let him into her life, and heart, if they continued to grow closer, by the time Christmas arrived, their every dream would finally come true.

AN HOUR LATER, they headed for the kitchen. Zane got them both some water, then pulled out a package of peppermint and white chocolate pretzel crisps. As they settled on the sofa in front of the fire, his gaze drifted over her, taking in every well-adored inch. "You look ravishing."

Nora fluffed her tousled hair and swept a hand down her still-tingling body and bare legs. "I think you mean *ravished*." Playfully, she let her eyes move over his bare chest and low-slung pajama pants. "Where did you get these anyway?"

He was wearing the Black Watch plaid bottoms of a pair of men's pajamas. She was wearing the notch-collared, buttoned-front top. Nice as they were—and they were made of the finest, softest flannel—they didn't seem exactly his style.

Zane opened up the bag and offered her first dibs. "My brothers gave them to me a couple of Christmases ago. Said that since I'd probably be an old man before I settled down, they wanted to go ahead and give me the appropriate nightwear."

"Cute."

He shook his head at the joking antics of his brothers. "Speaking of settling down, though, I do have something important I want to talk to you about."

As their eyes met and held, Nora felt a shimmer of tension between them. "Okay."

He sifted a hand through her hair. "Finding out about Liam was a wake-up call for me."

Doing her best to maintain a poker face, Nora ran a fingertip across the inside of his wrist. "In what way?"

He continued to study her with his steady gaze, as if trying to figure something out. Admitting finally, "I guess I always thought we would get back together again eventually. Even after our last breakup."

So did I, Nora thought on a wistful sigh.

He lifted her hand to his lips and pressed a kiss into the center of her palm. "Seeing you move on without me, creating a new life here, a new family, forced me to realize you weren't going to wait for me forever." His voice took on a husky undertone. "And I'd been a fool to think you would."

His heartbreak engendered her own. Nora shook her head. Why go back to that, if all it was going to do was hurt them both? "Zane…"

His eyes gleamed with undecipherable emotion. "Let me finish, Nora. Anyway, I didn't—don't—like the idea of you moving on without me." His voice dropped a husky notch. "And I especially don't want Liam to grow up without a man in his life he can count on."

Nora regarded Zane in shock.

Please tell me he's not going to propose out of some misguided sense of duty or honor…

As he gazed over at her, Nora had the strong sense he was thinking of kissing her again. But he did not.

Which was good. Because kissing would lead to touching and touching would lead to lovemaking, which would lead to even more confounding emotions than they already had.

He traced her lifeline with the pad of his thumb. "And

I really don't like the idea of you and Liam ever wanting or needing anything."

Palm tingling, she reiterated softly, "We don't." *Especially now that you're in our lives.*

"So I'm stepping up here. I started working on figuring out what to do with the inheritance my dad left me. As well as my will."

Oh, dear God. "Zane…" She knew how superstitious soldiers could be. Sometimes just preparing for death could lead them to believe the end was imminent.

"I've changed the beneficiary to my personal life insurance policy, and the one I get through the military, to benefit you and Liam. And when I get the stuff with the No Name all sorted out, I plan to add that to the inheritance, too."

Nora turned to face him directly. She gazed at him in consternation. "Does your family know this?"

He shook his head somberly. "Only the lawyer I hired in town. Plus, of course, the insurance people."

Nora lifted a trembling hand. "Zane. I appreciate the thought. But—" she gulped "—this is crazy."

Exuding his trademark confidence, he shifted her over onto his lap and cuddled her close. "Actually—" the corners of his lips quirked up "—I think it's the sanest thing I've done in a long while."

Worry combined with her guilt. "I don't want your money." She'd done nothing to earn it.

"Too bad." He buried his face in her hair, breathed in deeply. "Because I want you and Liam to have it."

Nora closed her eyes, too, praying for strength. "But your family…" How were they likely to take this? Yes, they welcomed her now, but if they thought she was a gold digger, how would they react?

"My family does not need any money from me." Zane

stroked a comforting hand down her spine. "They all have enough, on their own."

"That's really not the point," Nora murmured miserably.

"Yes," Zane countered, "it is." He cupped her chin, lifting her face to his. Gazing deep into her eyes, he said, "They want me to be happy, Nora. They know that you and Liam make me happy."

He made her happy, too.

"And since you are the closest thing to family outside the Lockharts that I have, let me honor that connection by looking after you and Liam. And in turn, you can take care of me." He kissed her tenderly.

"Through sex," Nora guessed, pulling in a stabilizing breath.

"That's one way." He leveled an assessing gaze on her and kept it there. "There are other ways, too, that are just as important."

She swallowed around the sudden ache in her throat. "Like…?"

"Just be there for me," he replied hoarsely, in a way that made her heart skip first one beat, then another. "Know I have to go back to active duty for a couple of weeks, after Christmas. But then I'll be home for good."

Unless, Nora thought, something happened somewhere in the world that required his services. But Zane wasn't allowing himself to entertain that possibility. Not in his mind. Not in his heart. Not yet.

Recklessly deciding to let the specter of reenlistment go, at least for now, she said softly, "And when you return?"

His expression turned even more sincere. He kissed her again, then advised, "Greet me with open arms, and an even more open heart."

ZANE AND NORA made love again, through the night. They got up at 4:00 a.m. with Liam, fed and diapered him, and then all went back to bed for another two hours' sleep. But then it was time to get up and figure out what they were going to do for the rest of the day.

"Since you're the one who is working, while I'm the one on R & R, you should probably get first dibs on the choice of activity during your day off," Zane said.

Nora sat with Liam on her lap. Still clad in his oversize pajama shirt and a pair of his thick wool hiking socks, she looked sexy and at ease. "Does that mean you're volunteering to come with?"

"I am." Zane paused to read the back of the pancake box. After a thoughtful squint and some mental calculating, he poured in half the packet of flour mix into the bowl.

"Do you want to measure that?" Nora asked, her hair tousled, cheeks still pink with sleep. She snuggled her son against her with a maternal tenderness that made something raw and elemental twist in his gut.

"Nah. I'm good." He broke two eggs into the bowl. Added a splash of milk and a couple spoonfuls of melted butter.

The truth was, he loved having them here. Knew the No Name would forever feel lonely without them.

But he was working on that. Hopefully, when Christmas got here, he would have everything in place.

In the meantime, he had two hungry "family members" to feed. He paused, looking at the fruit bowl on the counter and the containers of fresh berries in the fridge. "Blueberries or bananas?"

Nora smiled, as if enjoying the show. When he caught her admiring his physique, a faint blush stained her cheeks. "Blueberries."

Glad she wasn't as immune to him as she sometimes pretended to be, he sauntered closer. "Maple syrup or berry?"

Her sky blue eyes glowed happily. "Maple."

He walked over to brush a brief kiss on the top of her head, another on Liam's, then went back to the stove and turned on the griddle. "Back to what we were saying… about what you'd really like to do today?"

Nora sobered. "Well, although I've ordered a few things on the internet, I haven't had time to do any in-person shopping for Liam. So shopping would be nice."

"Consider it done." Zane poured her a glass of juice and handed it to her. "How far away do you want to go?"

She sent him a hopeful glance. "There's a new mega toy store in San Angelo. And they usually have a Santa Claus at the mall there."

The coziness factor in the room increased tenfold. "Sounds fun."

Her brows knit together. "What do you want to do?"

Aware he could really get used to this, Zane sent her a sidelong glance. "Whatever you want to do. The day is yours. And Liam's." He gave her a long meaningful look, then promised playfully, "My mission is seeing to your every need."

And what an adventure it turned out to be.

By the time they arrived at noon, the line for Santa was over an hour long. Zane looked at the fussy, impatient children and their equally out-of-sorts parents. "Want to come back?"

Nora bit her lip. "I don't think I'm going to get another chance."

Zane could see she really wanted to do this. "If you want to wheel Liam around in the stroller, I'll hold our place in line."

"You really don't mind?" she asked, coming intimately close.

He inhaled her lavender perfume. "I really don't mind."

And as it turned out, Zane didn't. Mostly because it gave him a little time to field two phone calls from Sage—who wanted to know if he had contacted her friend Raquel yet. Zane hadn't. And a couple of fellas from his unit, who demanded to know if he'd come to his senses. He had. Just not in the way his teammates wished. And last but not least, he used the time to research the hottest new toys for three-month-olds that holiday season.

Finally, it was almost their time. Zane looked around, spying Nora, waved her on over. They got Liam out of his stroller just as their turn came up. Beaming with excitement, Nora handed her son over to Santa.

Liam took one look at the big burly man with the snowy white beard and glasses, screwed up his face and let out a howl loud enough to alert the entire shopping center.

Nora rushed in to comfort him. To no avail.

"Maybe if you hold him up next to Santa," the woman dressed as Mrs. Claus mouthed.

Again, no dice. Liam was having none of it.

Nora gestured for Zane to try, too. That didn't work, either, so the photographer took several shots of the squalling red-faced baby in Santa's arms. They stayed long enough to pay and collect their freshly printed photos, and then moved off into the mall.

As soon as Santa's village was out of sight, Liam quieted.

Nora, however, remained frustrated and distraught. "Maybe it just wasn't the day for it," he soothed.

Nora's spine stiffened, even as she nodded.

"But we can still get in some shopping we wanted to do," Zane said, beginning to understand why some of the young families they saw all around them seemed so tense and out of sorts.

Luckily, by the time they got to the toy store, Liam was drowsy again. "Why don't you let me carry him while you shop?" Zane suggested.

She sent him a grateful glance. "You're sure?"

He admired the sunny highlights in her chestnut hair, the way the loose sexy waves just brushed her shoulders. "Actually, I'd really enjoy it." Having Liam in the BabyBjörn, nestled against his chest, made him feel like a dad. Liam's dad. And, Zane noted, there was no feeling better than that. Unless you considered also getting an idea of what it would be like to be Nora's husband...

"Well, that went better," she said, when at last they had finished at the toy store, and were loading their bagged purchases into the back of his minivan. She reached up to curve a gentle hand against Liam's cheek. Zane caught the brief, wistful look in her eyes. "Do you think we bought too much?"

Given the fact that, for every item she had purchased, he had insisted on getting something else?

He leaned down impulsively and bussed the top of Liam's head. Wrapping an arm around Nora's shoulders, he pulled her affectionately against his side. "Hey, I'm ready to go back in and clear out the rest of the store!"

She laughed, resting her head against his shoulder. Peering up at him contentedly, she reflected, "It's exciting, isn't it?"

More than Zane ever could have predicted. "I can only imagine what it's going to be like when he sees all his new toys."

Nora turned to him, a mixture of surprise and wary expectation on her lovely face. "You are going to be there with us. Aren't you?"

Chapter Eleven

"I'd sure like to be there with the two of you on Christmas morning," Zane said huskily, helping Nora settle Liam in his safety seat. Together, they buckled him in and directed his attention to the travel toys within his reach.

As they straightened, Zane caught a whiff of her lavender perfume and the sweet essence that was unique to her.

Nora tucked her hand in his and turned to him with a smile. "Maybe you could spend Christmas Eve with us, too? I mean," she added hastily, lest she overstep, "I imagine you have things you want to do with the Lockhart clan, too."

Aware this was what had been missing in his life, Zane leaned down and pressed his forehead to hers. "Nothing would make my family happier than to have you and Liam there with me, too."

Stepping back, she searched his face in relief. "What about you, soldier?" Her teasing tone held an undercurrent of uncertainty.

Was she kidding? He brought her to him, and kissed her tenderly. "I'm happier than I've ever been."

Nora snuggled against him. "Me, too," she whispered.

From inside the passenger compartment, Liam chortled loudly. Zane and Nora broke apart, laughing. "I think our tiny chaperone is telling us to get a move on," he remarked ruefully.

"I think you're right," Nora concluded, handing Zane the keys to her minivan.

He climbed behind the wheel. They were almost back to Laramie when Nora's phone chimed. She listened with what appeared to be a frown of concern. "Yes, I can be there. Zane, too. Probably fifteen minutes. See you then." She punched the end call button.

Zane tossed her a brief, concerned glance before returning his attention to the road. "Problem?"

Nora moaned. "The Ugly Sweater competition rules are going to be read during the dinner hour this evening. Our presence is requested."

Zane paused. "Why is that a big deal?"

Nora ran both her hands through her hair, then let them fall to her lap. "You only ask that because you haven't heard the rules."

Unable to help but note the way the tousled sun-streaked strands caught the winter light, he said, "Oh, man…"

She nodded, already exasperated. "Exactly."

"What else?" he prodded curiously.

She bent her head as she checked the messages on her phone. "Mr. Pierce's test results are in, and Dr. Wheeler wants to meet at Laramie Gardens ASAP to discuss them. So, if you can spare the time to sit in for that…"

"I'll be there as long as I'm needed."

"Thanks." She texted a reply. "I appreciate it."

He reached over and squeezed her knee. "No problem."

Twenty minutes later, Liam was being tended to in the community room by a doting Miss Mim, and Zane and Nora and Mr. Pierce were seated in the conference room with Dr. Wheeler.

The geriatric specialist had his laptop open and was showing them the MRI and CT scans. "As you can see," the doctor concluded, "there are no abnormalities."

"So I'm not ill?" Mr. Pierce asked incredulously.

The physician handed over a paper copy of the results. "We had two different teams look at the results. Neurology and geriatrics. The conclusion was unanimous. There's no evidence of stroke, tumor or disease. No diminished blood flow, or any other evidence of anything that would cause mental confusion."

Mr. Pierce slumped in his chair. "So why am I still having periods of confusion and disorientation? Short-term memory problems?"

Good question, Zane thought, as unsatisfied as the man he'd been drafted to support.

"That, we don't know yet," Dr. Wheeler said kindly. "All we can verify right now is that there is no underlying biological or physiological condition evident."

Which meant what? Zane wondered. That a time would come when they would find something nefarious in Mr. Pierce's brain?

The older man sat up straight in his chair. "What about medication? Isn't there something I can take that would help? I see advertisements all the time."

Most of which were quack cures, even Zane knew. Marketed and sold to the truly desperate.

His manner firm yet soothing, Dr. Wheeler replied, "We're not recommending adding anything else to your daily regimen at this point. We'd rather focus on other options like occupational therapy. Daily physical activity and memory exercises. Perhaps a better, much more specific daily schedule to keep you on track."

"I can make arrangements to get you started on all that tomorrow," Nora put in.

Mr. Pierce traced the buckle on the classic leather-bound copy of *Treasure Island* in front of him. He looked up warily. "And if that doesn't work?"

Dr. Wheeler frowned. "Then we'll have to consider *at least discussing* moving you to a place that focuses specifically on memory care."

WHILE NORA STAYED behind to speak with Dr. Wheeler, Zane walked down the hall with Mr. Pierce. His heart went out to the eighty-five-year-old. "Not exactly what you wanted to hear?"

Mr. Pierce shook his head, disappointed. They continued on a moment in silence. "You know what I did last night? I spent an hour looking for my wallet."

"Where was it?" Zane asked.

"In my trousers pocket," he related, embarrassed.

Zane clapped a hand on his shoulder, empathizing. "We all do that. I can't tell you the number of times I've lost my sunglasses only to find out they were on my head."

As they entered his suite, Mr. Pierce continued grimly, "You know what I did at *midnight* on *Friday*?"

Zane shook his head, waiting for the older man to enlighten him.

"I called the owner of the Rare Books Store in Wichita Falls, a colleague I've known and worked with for thirty years, and berated him for not having sent Esther's Christmas gift, which was a gold-leaf embossed leather-bound edition of *Little Women*. Sort of like this one." Mr. Pierce held up *Treasure Island*. "Only without the buckle."

Zane took the seat Mr. Pierce suggested. "What did your colleague do?"

He shelved his book with the other classics in his vast collection. Then returned to sit in the armchair opposite Zane. "Well, at first my friend thought I was joking, since he knows as well as I do that Esther is in heaven. And then when he realized I wasn't, he played along with me. And then called Lynn in New York City."

"I'm guessing your daughter then called you?"

"Yes. Hearing her voice snapped me out of it, and I told her I thought I'd been sleepwalking."

"Lynn doesn't know the problems you've been having?"

Russell Pierce frowned. "Nurse Nora informed her about my occcassional confusion the first couple of weeks that I lived here. Lynn was so concerned I haven't let anyone here tell her anything since."

Which was his right, Zane knew, under medical privacy laws.

"But if this keeps up, my daughter will figure it out. Perhaps sooner rather than later, since she is planning to come down for Christmas to visit me."

Zane looked him in the eye. "How can I help?"

"That's just it. You can't." Russell frowned. "If I'm going to snap myself out of this foggy mess I've been living in, I'm going to have to do it myself."

"IS MR. PIERCE OKAY?" Nora asked worriedly as Zane caught up with her and Liam. She watched the elderly gentleman walk into the dining hall and take a seat at a table with Wilbur Barnes and Darrell Enlow. He seemed alert and aware. Determinedly cheerful. As if his private talk with Zane had helped somehow. Nora knew how that felt. There was just something so kind and reassuring about him. She always felt better, just being with him.

He turned to Nora, gave her shoulder a squeeze.

"I think so." Zane paused in obvious concern, relating quietly, "He's frustrated, of course."

Nora sighed. "We all are. I had hoped the tests would show something really minor that could be fixed instead of just…nothing." She shook her head.

"Maybe the memory therapies you are setting up for him will help."

Glad she had Zane to lean on in that moment, Nora bit her lip. "Maybe. I just can't help but think we're letting him down somehow, though."

Zane met her gaze. "What else could you have done?"

That was just it. She shook her head in silent admonition. "I don't know." She swallowed around the knot of emotion in her throat. "I'm going to have to think on it some more. Talk to Dr. Wheeler again." She gestured to the front of the dining hall, where Betty Blair and Miss Patricia were waving at them. "In the meantime, I think they've reserved some seats for us."

Zane grinned. "We better get up there then before someone has a conniption."

She ran her gaze over his tall, muscular frame. In jeans, boots and a charcoal crewneck sweater that brought out the dark silver of his eyes, he was the epitome of rugged masculinity. "It's your fault. If you weren't so genial and capable, you wouldn't be so popular."

He tossed her an amused glance, then tilted his handsome head in the direction of her adorable baby boy, currently commanding a similar amount of feminine attention. "Actually, I think it's Liam they're after, darlin'."

Nora chuckled. "Could be."

A cute infant was a hot commodity in a seniors' center.

They made their way and sat down, just as Miss Sadie took the podium. "Okay, everyone, we're going to run through the rules for the Ugly Sweater contest," she announced, as papers stating the same were passed out by the dining hall aides.

"Every sweater must be a base color of green or red."

From the look on Zane's face, it was all he could do not to moan.

Nora nudged his knee beneath the table.

Gave him a look that said *behave*.

Mischief glittering in his eyes, he nudged her knee right back.

"Homemade decals or decorations must adorn the front and/or the sleeves, while the backs of the sweaters are to be left plain."

As Miss Sadie went on, with the exact dimensions and type of fabric or material permissible for each decoration, Zane's eyes began to glaze over a little. He looked distracted. Restless. Worse, Nora couldn't blame him for being bored.

This was a little much.

Even more so for someone in the Special Forces, where high stakes, fast action and adrenaline were the norm.

His phone chimed softly. Looking stoked for the interruption, he removed it from his pocket and put it down on his thigh, where only he could see the screen.

Frowning, he discreetly texted something back. Then put the phone back in his pocket.

It went off again, ever so softly.

And then again.

He answered briefly—twice—then put it back in his pocket.

Nora was curious. And so was Betty Blair, who was seated on the other side of him.

Was it someone from his unit? Nora wondered, as the texts continued nonstop. His family? And why did Zane suddenly look so completely engrossed and businesslike…? As if he had the weight of the world on his shoulders?

Oblivious to whatever was going on with Zane and the messages he was receiving, and the way Betty Blair was practically breaking her neck trying to figure it out, too, Miss Sadie concluded, "So those are the rules. And just like last year, we'll have three impartial judges from the community, unless there are any objections." She lowered her bifocals. "Yes, Betty?"

"I think Nora needs to participate this year." Betty paused to give Zane a long, meaningful look. As if blaming him for his complete lack of attention during this very important holiday event. "Zane, too."

A murmur of assent went through the hall. What was the older woman up to? Nora wondered. More matchmaking? Or simply an attempt to draw Zane more fully into life at Laramie Gardens.

Nora lifted her hand. "Actually, I don't think it would be fair for me to compete against any of the residents."

This time, Zane nudged her foot with his. "Actually—" he looked at her, his preoccupation with his texts fading, a mischievous twinkle in his eyes "—I think it's only fair you do compete, Nora."

Everyone chuckled.

"Liam could enter, too!" Miss Patricia said excitedly.

Which would really make it seem like the three of them were officially a family. Suddenly, life in Laramie was getting far too complicated.

"If I do it, and Liam does it, you have to do it, too, Zane Lockhart," Nora declared, just as emphatically, wondering how in the world she was going to find the time to make two sweaters before the deadline the following week. Never mind compete with Zane!

The incorrigible lieutenant folded his arms across his

broad chest and flashed her a hallelujah smile. Then he leaned toward her and winked, as if he couldn't wait. "You're on!"

"So NOW DO you see what you got yourself into?" Nora asked, several hours later, after Liam was finally asleep in his crib.

Sighing dramatically, Zane studied the contest regulations with a jaundiced eye. "That's a lot of rules," he said finally.

Nora continued putting ornaments on her tree, aware at the rate she was going, her house would not be fully decorated for the holidays until Christmas Eve. But she couldn't really say she minded her slow-as-a-turtle pace, given the reason behind it. All the time spent with Liam. And Zane.

Trying not to dwell on the fact that his R & R was now more than half over, Nora continued her mock scolding, "Which you would have known had you been paying more attention when Miss Sadie was reading them." *Instead of managing whatever it was you were overseeing on your cell phone.*

Zane put aside the competition explanation, then ambled toward her. He picked up several ornaments and began placing them on the branches. The faint restlessness he'd evidenced all evening was still there. Only now it was directed right at her. "What happens if you don't follow the contest rules?" he asked slyly.

Or, she wondered, *you find you can't handle the much-slower pace of a small Texas town, after all?*

Their shoulders brushed as they both moved in the same direction at once. Nora worked to still her racing pulse and stepped back so they were no longer touching. She met his gaze equably. "You get disqualified."

And I get my heart broken all over again, just as I sort of always knew I would.

"How about that," Zane murmured, grinning as if he'd just found a way out of the situation he didn't really want to be in.

Hoping the Ugly Sweater contest wasn't a metaphor for the situation they always eventually found themselves in, Nora frowned. "You need to take this seriously, soldier, now that you've gotten us all in it," she warned, going back to the box for more ornaments.

Because she would be here, living in Texas and working at Laramie Gardens, long after he had left again.

If he reenlisted again.

He *said* he wouldn't.

She knew he *wanted* to believe that. And most of his current actions pointed to that. But she also knew what had happened before, when he'd been needed by his country. He'd gone off to serve. The possibility he might do so again remained, whether either of them wanted to admit it or not. Because there was always a crisis somewhere in the world, an American citizen or soldier who needed rescuing. Always a need for his elite Special Forces unit. And within that, a need for a talented soldier like Zane.

"You can't duck out of this competition," she said sternly. "Not after promising to be in it."

Abruptly reminding her of the way he and his fellow elite operators liked to blow off steam, he regarded her in all innocence. "Not planning to."

Yeah, right. He was formulating a strategy. Most likely an ornery one to liven up what otherwise had the potential to be a very nitpicky and tedious event. She peered at him suspiciously, demanding, "What are you planning?"

Zane picked up the last of the colored glass bulbs. He placed his on the highest branches, filling in the places she had thus far been unable to reach. "I'm going to surprise you."

Exactly what she feared. She needed predictable. She needed safe. She needed him here, with her and Liam.

Smile widening, he clasped her wrist and reeled her in. "And speaking of surprises..."

She quirked a brow, prompting him to elaborate.

"Now that we finally have your tree decorated," he said in that deep, husky voice she loved, "do you want to wrap Liam's presents tonight?"

Something else they'd put off.

Something else that would make them feel even more like a family. One that, despite all her secret hopes and dreams, she wasn't sure was going to last.

"On one condition," Nora countered, before she could stop herself, recalling how elusive and distracted he'd been most of that evening.

Zane's brow lifted the way it always did when unsolicited conditions were put on him.

"You tell me who Raquel is."

Chapter Twelve

Zane stared at Nora. "How do you know about Raquel?" he asked incredulously.

"Betty Blair was reading your text messages all through dinner. You seriously didn't notice?"

He shrugged. "I only had eyes for you and Liam."

"And your phone," Nora couldn't resist adding.

"True," he said a bit sheepishly.

She held his gaze. Waited.

He came closer. Reluctantly admitted, "Raquel is a friend of Sage's. Someone from our family's Dallas days. She's agreed to help me out with an estate matter."

Nora knew, from her own grandparents' passing, how complicated and seemingly unending the legal matters could be after the loss of a loved one. And given his family's extensive wealth, it was probably even more so.

She flushed, embarrassed to have put him on the spot like that. "Oh."

Gently, he cupped her face in his large, warm palm. "So there really is no need for you to be jealous."

Nora released an uneven breath. "I'm not!"

His brow lifted in a way that said it was his turn to await a response. Unfortunately, Nora couldn't explain it in a way that would not make her sound overly mistrustful. She just had a nagging feeling Zane was holding something back from her.

The clandestine talk with his brother during the dinner at the Circle H, with Garrett requesting Zane not speak to their mom about Zane's plans until after Christmas Day. The big stack of papers Zane was trying to go through, at long last. His changing the beneficiary on his life insurance policies to make sure she and Liam were taken care of, in the event of anything happening to him.

It was all a little too much. All seeming to point to one thing. He was likely going to reenlist for another tour, leave her again for months at a time and let his service to his country dictate the terms of his life.

He was being noble. Courageous.

Whereas she was worried and upset. With effort, she pushed her anxiety away. What good would it do to fret about any of this now, when he only had some twelve days left before he returned to finish his tour? They still had Christmas together.

Maybe it was time she started doing what she had promised herself and start living more in the moment, too. Give him the space he needed to really figure out just what he was going to do next, and then simply support him. Instead of always agonizing about what lay just beyond the bend.

Maybe it was time she dug deep to find a wellspring of courage and selflessness, too.

"I'm sorry. It's been a long day." She swallowed around the ache in her throat. "I'm just exhausted."

Holding her gaze, he rubbed his thumb across her lower lip. "Do you still want to wrap presents, then, while Liam's asleep, or call it a day so you can go on to bed?"

"Actually," Nora said, taking him all the way in her arms. "What I'd really like to do is this."

ZANE GRINNED AS Nora tugged off his sweater, then took him by the hand and up to her bed. With a sweeping gesture, she invited him to sit on the edge while she began a slow and seductive striptease.

Apparently, it was his turn for Christmas to come early. He watched her undress, the sight of her extraordinarily intimate and immensely pleasurable.

Tempestuous need glittered in her eyes, as clad only in a very sexy red silk bra and panties, she drew him to his feet and slowly removed his shirt. "I thought you were tired."

Her hands divested him of the last of his clothes, then closed over his pulsing hardness. "Not that tired."

Playfully, he drew the bra straps down over her arms, exposing her erect nipples. "So I see."

She stretched out, facing him on the bed. Smiling as he eased his fingers beneath the elastic and found her damp, silky, waiting. Wanting. Bent to kiss the curve of her bare shoulder. Grinning lustily, she observed, "You're not too tired, either."

"I'm never too tired to make love with you." He'd never stop wanting her, needing her, either.

Determined to make this lovemaking more memorable than anything they'd ever had, he eased the lingerie from her body and rolled so she was beneath him. Positioned himself between her thighs. She came up off the bed as his lips lowered, suckling gently. Her thighs fell even farther apart as he kissed and stroked. Until she shuddered and fell to pieces in his arms.

And only when she could stand it no longer did he slide inside her, in one smooth languid stroke. She clenched around him as he filled her completely, taking him and making him hers. Letting him possess her, hold her and love her, until there was no more denying how much she wanted and needed him in her life. Until the future was theirs, too, for the taking.

All he had to do, Zane thought, as their shudders ended, and they lay together, cuddling, was complete the mission he had embarked on this Christmas.

The mission that would bring both Nora and Liam into his life from here on out.

Unfortunately, there was still a lot to do to make it all happen, he thought, as he stroked a hand through her hair. "I probably should go," he said.

"Stay," she murmured, pressing a string of sleepy kisses across his chest. "Just a little while longer…"

He didn't have to be asked twice. Reveling in the feel of her lissome body entwined with his, Zane shut his eyes. The next thing he knew it was midnight. He had stayed past the time he should. And the bed beside him was empty.

He rose and pulled on his pants. Went down the hall to the nursery. Liam was still sleeping peacefully in his crib. There was no sign of Nora.

He found her downstairs sitting on the sofa, her laptop in front of her. Clad in a long-sleeved, red T-shirt and matching flannel pajama bottoms, her chestnut hair falling in a loose braid over one shoulder, her lips still swollen from their kisses, she looked gorgeous, well-loved. And worried.

Tamping down the desire to draw her into his arms and make love to her all over again, he sat down next to her. "Everything okay?"

She turned a troubled glance his way. "I couldn't sleep. I keep thinking about Mr. Pierce."

Zane wasn't surprised. The elderly man had been on their minds a lot lately. "Still feel like you're missing something?"

Nora nodded. "There's always a reason why symptoms appear. We can't always find it or identify it, but it's usually buried somewhere in the patient's medical history."

"I thought you and Dr. Wheeler had been all through this."

Nora exhaled. "Numerous times. The signs all point to sundowning, and perhaps the very, very early signs of dementia or Alzheimer's."

"But you don't agree?"

"No." She tapped her index finger against her lips. "And I don't know if it's my gut instinct kicking in, the fact I knew Mr. Pierce all those years growing up, that is making me think his intermittent confusion and disorientation is caused by something else that is eminently treatable."

She shook her head miserably. "Or if it's because I *am* so fond of him that I am refusing to accept what could, in time, become a hopelessly demoralizing and discouraging diagnosis."

Denial was tough. He had been in his own form of it for years now. He took her free hand in his and lifted it to his lips. "So what next?"

Nora reluctantly shut the lid of her computer. "I talk with Mr. Pierce tomorrow. Go over what we know and see if I can find something we might have inadvertently overlooked."

"Is ZANE COMING in today?" Miss Isabelle asked the following day, while Nora passed out the morning medications to the residents already in the dining hall for breakfast.

"No," she said, recalling how passionately they had made love before he left. "He had to go to Dallas for a few days."

"So close to Christmas?" Miss Patricia frowned.

"I bet it has something to do with that Raquel person." Betty Blair glowered.

Actually, it did. But, not about to go into that with them, Nora simply smiled. Trying not to feel defensive, even though Zane was still keeping an awful lot from her, she said, "Let's not forget Zane did grow up there and still has a lot of friends living in that area," she pointed out reasonably. "Second, whatever Zane's reason, it's his business, don't you think?"

"As long as he comes back in plenty of time to spend Christmas with Liam and you, Nora," Miss Sadie said with an elegant smile.

The constant matchmaking was both heartwarming and exasperating. Knowing, however, the LG residents only had her best interests in mind, Nora reminded everyone gently, "He has plans with his family, too."

"Are you invited?" Miss Mim inquired hopefully.

"Yes." She blushed, trying not to make too much of that. Although she could see everyone else was. "And I'm sure he will also find time to swing by here to wish everyone a merry Christmas, too."

"What about the Ugly Sweater contest?" Betty Blair asked.

"He was reading the rules for it just last evening."

"So he is going to enter!" Miss Patricia swallowed her meds.

He was going to have to, since he had also roped Liam and Nora into it. "Absolutely," Nora promised. Then headed down the hall to check on Mr. Pierce.

He was still in his pajamas and wearing slippers. His robe was hanging over the back of the chair next to his bed. Not particularly good signs. "Are you cold?" Nora asked, wondering why he had his winter coat on, too.

"No." Russell Pierce patted his empty pockets. "Just looking for my car keys."

Oh, dear, he was confused again. In the morning, too! Usually he was fine in the morning. Nora gently touched his arm. "You don't drive anymore, Mr. Pierce. Remember?"

"Sure I do. Our minivan is in the..." He stopped. Looked at his clothing and sat down on the edge of the bed. He picked up the leather-bound edition of *Great Expectations* and idly fingered the clasp. Muttered something heartfelt that Nora was just as glad not to be able to decipher.

She poured him a glass of water from the pitcher at his bedside table and handed him the plastic cup holding his morning medications.

He took them.

"Is this a good time for us to talk?"

Mr. Pierce nodded.

Nora pulled up a chair. "First, I want you to know that the occupational therapist who is going to be working with you on memory exercises is coming at four this afternoon. The physical therapist will be here tomorrow. And we hope to have your more structured daily routine in place by the end of the week."

Looking oriented again, Mr. Pierce nodded. "Thank you, Nora. I appreciate all you're doing."

"You're welcome. Do you mind if we discuss your medical history for a moment? I was going over your pharmacy records last night, and I had a few questions."

"I'll answer anything I can."

"I appreciate that." She referred to the notes on her clipboard. "The last time you had any changes in your medication was last summer, when you started a new daily antihistamine. Do you remember why you made the switch from the one you had been taking? You were in New York City at the time."

"I had a couple of sinus infections earlier in the year, related to my pollen allergies. So the doc there thought the newest latest greatest thing might be the ticket to get rid of them."

"How did you react to it?"

"Fine."

"Have you had any sinus infections since?"

"Not a one."

Nora made another note. "And nothing else has been prescribed for you?"

"No. The doctors figure with my cholesterol, blood pressure and allergy medications, I've got enough going on."

"And when did your memory issues start?"

He grinned. "I can't recall."

Nora paused. "Are you joking, or…?"

Russell Pierce sobered. "Actually, I don't really know. Esther always said I only remembered the things I wanted to remember, and she was right. I only half listened most of the time." He looked sad again.

"And your move to New York last summer? What prompted that exactly?"

"I had locked myself out of my house a couple of times and misplaced my wallet and lost all my ID, and my daughter didn't want me living alone anymore."

Nora paused. Aware this wasn't in her records. "So you were having memory issues before the move?"

"Yes, but—" briefly his expression became prickly "—no more than I had always had. I tended to do that a couple of times a year anyway. But Lynn was concerned and wanted to spend more time with me, so I let her talk me into it."

Nodding, Nora wrapped up with a few more questions.

Satisfied Mr. Pierce was alert and aware again, she left him to dress unassisted and went back to her office.

The rest of the day was very busy. By the time she finished up for the day and collected Liam, the excitement over the Ugly Sweater competition was at full pitch.

"You better have something really wild to show everyone," Nora said when Zane called her from Dallas that evening.

"I don't know about wild. How about simply *memorable*?" he teased.

Nora groaned, still wishing he were here with her, instead of over one hundred and fifty miles away. "I hope your sense of humor matches the Laramie Gardens residents', soldier."

He chuckled. "How was Liam this evening?"

"Good."

"I missed seeing him."

"He missed seeing you." Her son had gotten used to having two adults around at bedtime, to help with the bathing and feeding, rocking and cuddling and story time.

Zane exhaled. The sound seemed to carry all the loneliness she was feeling. "I missed seeing you, too," he said.

Same here, was on the tip of Nora's tongue. But something, some inner vulnerability, wouldn't let her say it. If she got all emotional, she could start crying and really feeling sorry for herself.

And that would not be good.

For either of them.

"When will you be home? I mean," she corrected hastily, "back in Laramie County?"

He let her remark go unchallenged. "Thursday morning," he said cheerfully.

"The day after tomorrow."

Which meant another day and night, and maybe day alone.

How was she going to survive without seeing him, being with him, making love to him every day?

"What you're doing must be complicated," she said, opening the door for him to tell her more.

To her frustration, he chose not to elaborate about that. Instead, said with his usual cheerfulness, "As long as I am in Dallas, however, I was wondering. Nora, what did you ask Santa for this year?"

Zane. With a big red bow on him. And a lifetime guarantee. Glad he wasn't there to see her blush, Nora fibbed, "Mmm. I don't know."

He chuckled, deep and low.

Her entire body tingled in response. And missed him all the more.

"Everyone should have *something* to open on Christmas morning," he said.

She knew that. And yet… Nora looked at her beautifully lit and decorated tree, struggling to contain her emotions. "We've never been really big on presents in my family."

His voice took on a more determined edge. "Maybe it's time that changed."

Nora couldn't contain a self-effacing laugh. "Good luck convincing Davina and The General of that." She paused as the silence drew out, wishing Zane were there with her and could take her in his strong arms and offer all the comfort and joy she needed right then.

Nora dragged in a calming breath. "Did I tell you that I heard from my mom, via text message, and Davina was right? Our mom wanted me to buy and wrap something for Liam from her, too?"

"She's not planning to come down for Christmas at all?" Zane did not sound happy.

Nora shrugged and tried not to feel bitter. "Maybe in the spring, she said."

Zane was silent. They weren't FaceTiming, so she couldn't see his expression. And for once she was glad of that. She didn't want to view his pity. It was enough to hear it in the awkward silence still stretching between them.

"Jewelry?"

"What?" she said, her mind still on the gregarious warmth of his family. He was so lucky to have the Lockharts in his corner. She wondered if he knew it.

"I need you to give me a *category*," he said.

A frisson of fear trickled through her. Presents would make everything seem traditional, and they both knew their relationship was anything but the norm. "You really don't have to do that," she returned.

"I really *want* to do that." His voice dropped a sexy, affectionate notch. "So…jewelry? Don't all women love jewelry?"

They loved wedding and engagement and eternity rings.

But she couldn't say that, either. Not without boxing him into a corner. And they both knew how much he hated that.

No, if Zane ever wanted to be with her and Liam, he would have to decide to do so on his own. Not be regimented into it. In the meantime, she needed to work on changing her own attitude. Becoming all that she could be in the mom and not-quite-a-girlfriend, not-quite-a-wife, but-a-heck-of-a-lot-more-than-a-simple-friend-or-lover category. "Maybe something Mom-ish," she said finally.

"Like a locket?"

Or a wedding ring.

She really had to stop this. Wishing for the impossible. Even if it was Christmastime! "Or a broach with birthstones," Nora said, "like my grandmother used to wear."

She could almost hear him smile. With pleasure. Or was that relief? "Liam would probably like that," Zane said.

He'd like us married even more, Nora thought.

But that wasn't likely to happen. Not with Zane leaving again. And even if he did ask, she wasn't entirely sure she could say yes. Even if it was what she wanted, deep down. Not when she knew he was just going to walk out the door. Not when she knew being married to him was only likely to leave her feeling even more lonely and disappointed when he did the inevitable and reenlisted.

"Nora…?" Zane prodded.

"Liam probably would like that. Very much. The question is, soldier, what do you want?"

"You, Nora," he said in that husky, sexy way of his that made her catch her breath. "Just you."

Chapter Thirteen

"What's all the noise?" Zane asked over the phone the next afternoon.

"I'm chaperoning a field trip to the fabric and craft stores," Nora explained.

"Ah. The Ugly Sweater contest."

She could hear voices on his end, too. Low and businesslike, unlike the ones on her end, which were high-pitched and peppered with eager laughter. "Everyone is getting pretty excited."

"Sounds like it."

Nora sifted through the stacks on the table, picking out a sweater her size, then Liam's. Putting both into a basket. "Anyway, I called to see if you want me to pick up one of the green or red cotton sweaters the craft store just got in."

"No." The smile remained in his voice. "I'm good."

He was in Dallas, where shopping options abounded. Figuring she might as well ask, as long as she was there, she said, "Did you need anything else? Fabric glue? Felt? Glitter? Jingle bells? Extra mistletoe?"

He chuckled. "Maybe the latter..."

Nora flushed at the veiled suggestiveness in his low tone.

The noises in the background faded. "So how are things with you?" Zane asked.

I miss you, Nora thought. Even though it had only been thirty-eight hours, five minutes and a few seconds since they had last seen each other. And less than twelve since they had last spoken on the phone. She rummaged through several spools of satin ribbon. "I'm good," she said. Or as good as she could get without Zane.

"Liam?"

He misses you, too. "Also good." She pretended a chipper attitude she couldn't quite feel.

"How is Mr. Pierce doing?"

"Another rough evening." Russell had wanted to see his late wife and had gotten agitated when she told him why that was not possible. Later, when he had finally understood, he'd become unbearably sad again.

As sad as Nora knew she would be if something happened to Zane, and their earthly connection ended.

"But he's better this morning," she forced herself to continue. And had been up and surfing the web on his computer tablet before breakfast, one of his beloved leather-bound classics sitting on the desk beside him.

The background noise on Zane's end faded even more. She could imagine him slipping away from whatever was going on to get a little more privacy. "Did you hear back yet on the antihistamine you were researching?" he asked.

"No," she admitted regretfully, doing the same thing and heading for a more deserted part of the store. She sighed. "But I've made queries at a dozen different places, so hopefully, something soon."

"Hopefully before Christmas."

"I know. Speaking of the holiday, is there anything on your gift list that this 'Santa' should know about?" She still had no idea what she was going to get him. Although she'd been thinking about some sort of Good Luck charm. Something to carry with him.

"Just one thing." His voice was a low, sexy rumble.

Her whole body tingling in response, Nora murmured back, "I'm listening."

"Wait up for me when I get back tomorrow night?"

THE FOLLOWING EVENING at ten o'clock, a rap sounded on Nora's front door. Pretending like she hadn't been waiting impatiently all evening for her gentleman caller, she sashayed to the door.

Zane stood on the other side of the door, a Santa hat on his head, a small gift-wrapped present in his hand. She couldn't help but laugh as she rose on tiptoe, kissed him hello, then ushered him inside.

He shrugged out of his coat, kissed her again, infusing her with the taste of peppermint this time, then lifted his head. Taking her hand, he led her over to the sofa, where she had a bottle of wine waiting. "Sorry it took me so long to get here."

He looked tired beneath the exuberant exterior. Like whatever it was he'd been doing had sapped the energy from him. Not an easy feat, with someone as unstoppable as Zane. "Traffic?"

She poured him a glass, then one for herself.

"No." He toasted her silently. "Just some things to wrap up in Dallas."

"Ah."

He picked up the present he'd brought in with him and handed it to her. It just covered the palm of her hand. "And of course I had to stop and get this."

Nora recognized the name of an exclusive store on the gift wrap. "What is it?"

Zane leaned back and folded his hands behind his head. "Open it and see."

Nora's heart skittered in her chest. "You don't want me to wait until Christmas morning?"

He tilted his head, considering. Eyes twinkling mysteriously, predicted, "You might like to have it now."

Now she really was curious. Nora took off the paper. Inside was a velvet jewelry box. Too big to be a ring, too square to be a bracelet or necklace.

Telling herself she was glad it wasn't an engagement ring, she lifted the lid.

Inside was an incredibly beautiful Christmas tree broach, with a pile of colorful, gaily wrapped presents underneath. In the center of each ribbon-tie was a gem.

Confidently, Zane explained, "Sapphire for Liam. Amethyst for you. Emerald for me. And see, there's even a couple extra presents in case you want to add a few more birthstones…"

For more children? *Their children*? Or was she really going off the rails now?

Nora blinked back tears. "It's beautiful, Zane."

"I'm glad you like it."

Silence fell.

"But…?" he asked, sensing there was more.

Nora dragged in another quavering breath. Almost afraid to ask, but needing to anyway. "Is there a special meaning in this?"

His gaze gentled. He pinned the broach on her, then cupped her face in both hands. "What do you think?"

"I think…" *I'm in love with you*, Nora thought.

But wary of inundating him with too much too soon, or putting a boundary on him he didn't want, she rose and went to the center drawer of her desk. Pulled out another jewelry box. "I think I need to give you this now, too." Even though it wasn't wrapped.

He stared down at the solid silver chain and pendant. "St. Michael the Archangel. The patron saint of soldiers and battles."

Nora looped it over his neck. "So you'll be protected wherever you go, whatever you're doing." Nora's voice turned rusty. "And know I'm thinking of you."

He took her all the way into his arms. "Without a doubt," he told her raggedly, "this is the best gift I've ever received."

Their lips met. He kissed her deeply, passionately, and in a masterful move, lifted her into his arms and swept her up the stairs to her bedroom. Then he carried her over to her bed and laid her down.

Parting her knees with his, he draped himself over her and situated himself between her thighs.

"Wow," she teased, "you must have really missed me."

"Darlin', you have no idea…" he growled, taking a wrist in each hand and anchoring them over her head. "But you will," he promised, kissing her mouth, slowly, sensually, and with breathtaking intensity.

He kissed her until they were both shuddering. Until she arched up against him and kissed him back with every inch of her being, until she shook with need, until their bodies melded in boneless pleasure.

They came apart long enough to undress each other and sheath him in a condom, then came together once again. He slid a pillow beneath her hips. They locked eyes, and she opened herself up to him as completely, as unconditionally as she knew how. He opened himself up to her in return, still kissing her feverishly, sliding home.

He lifted her against him, and suddenly she was there. Shattering in overwhelming release. And he was there, too. Clasping her to him. Joining her. Holding her close until the aftershocks faded. And when it was over she did not let him go, but instead, enticed him into making love with her again. Even more tenderly this time.

Afterward, they cuddled together, falling asleep. But at two in the morning, she woke to see him sitting up on the side of the bed. Reaching for his jeans.

Her hair tumbling over her bare shoulders, she rose up on her elbow. "You have to leave?"

Expression maddeningly inscrutable, he shrugged on his shirt. "I've got some stuff at the No Name to take care of first thing tomorrow morning."

Like what? she wondered. She grabbed her robe and followed him down the stairs. "Did you finally decide what you want to do with the land?"

He sat down on the bottom of the stairs to put on his socks, boots. "Keep it, I hope."

"Make it your home."

He rose to his full height, wrapped his arms around her waist and leaned over to kiss her. One corner of his mouth crooked mysteriously. "Let's just say, like a lot of things, it's a work in progress."

Or in other words, don't ask, Nora thought on a beleaguered sigh, feeling shut out all over again. "Afraid of jinxing it?"

"Maybe. Then again, maybe not."

She groaned and put her hands over her ears.

He pulled them off. Leaned down and waited until she'd dare look into his eyes, then bent down and kissed her again. Even more seductively this time. He tucked a strand of hair behind her ear. "Good things come to those who wait. Haven't you ever heard that?"

"Yes," Nora pouted, hating how fast their time together was flying by. How soon he would have to return to his unit, at least until he had finished his tour on January 15. "It doesn't mean I like it."

Zane reached for his coat.

"Do you really have to go?" She pouted even more as he shrugged it over his broad shoulders. He had done this before. Started pulling away emotionally before being deployed. She linked her arm through his as he headed for the door. "You could stay a few hours."

He studied her, clearly torn about something. "Don't you have to work tomorrow?"

Darn him for pointing that out. "Yes, but…"

His gaze drifted over her before returning ever so slowly to her face. "Nora wants what Nora wants?"

If he only knew. She folded her arms in front of her. "Exactly."

Zane exhaled heavily. Pulled her into his arms once again. "Believe me," he said, smoothing a hand over her back, "I'd like nothing better than to sleep right here all night."

She splayed her hands across his chest. "Then why don't you?"

"It's been pointed out to me it is not good for your reputation."

"By…?"

"Does it matter? They're right."

Nora hated it when he was right, too. Which made her take the opposite tack. Especially when their days together were numbered. She curved her hands over his biceps. "I really don't care what people think," she said stubbornly.

Zane paused, thinking. "It won't always be this way," he promised finally.

"But for right now?"

She looked in his eyes and knew it definitely was.

"I DON'T UNDERSTAND why we haven't seen Zane at all this week," Miss Sadie said, the following day.

I'm with you. I've missed him, too, Nora thought, as she finished updating a half dozen medical records. "He was in Dallas, taking care of Lockhart family business."

"But he's back now, isn't he?" Miss Mim persisted from the doorway of Nora's office.

"Yes." Nora shut down her computer. She walked across the hall and into the community room, where a lot of the residents were gathered. "And he's still busy."

"I think this has something to do with that Raquel person." Betty sniffed, following along.

"I think we should be grateful for everything that young man did when he was here." Miss Isabelle looked up from the drawing she and her little visitor, Braden Lockhart, were coloring.

No one could deny that.

The Adopt a Grandparent program was starting to take off and they had Zane to thank for getting the ball rolling. She would be eternally grateful to him for that.

Kurtis Kelley and Wilbur Barnes were engaged in an impromptu Battleship board game tournament with several middle school students in the community room.

High school choir students were setting up for a rehearsal of their annual holiday concert material in the music area.

Darrell Enlow was speaking with a fifth grader, who was doing a social studies report on what it had been like to serve in the military forty years prior.

"The point is, we'd like to thank him," Miss Sadie said. "So we all got together to give him this." She handed Nora a tabletop Christmas tree, decorated with lights and ornaments.

"We'd like you to deliver it to him," Betty added.

Nora would love to but she might be interrupting whatever he was so busy with. She smiled, suggesting, "Why don't you-all save it and give it to him yourselves during the Ugly Sweater contest?"

The women exchanged concerned looks.

"We want him to have it today," Betty insisted, consulting the wall clock. "And since you're just about finished for the day…"

Nora smiled as her sitter, Shanda, came toward her with Liam in her arms. "You want me to drive all the way out to the No Name ranch?"

Miss Patricia laid a hand over her heart. "Unless you want us all to go in the Activity Bus?"

"Seriously, Nora," Betty said, "you need to keep an eye on that man of yours if you don't want him to get away again. So if you don't do it, we will."

Nora could see the women meant it. So, even though she knew it wasn't necessary, she accepted the gift for Zane, then officially clocked out of work. With her sitter's help, she situated Liam in her minivan and drove out to the No Name.

She wasn't sure what she expected to see when she arrived at Zane's ranch. But it sure as heck wasn't what she found. A property clogged with vehicles of all sorts. Survey stakes dotted not just along the perimeter of the property, but within it, too. Worse, Zane did not look particularly happy to see her and Liam.

Realizing it had been a mistake to come without calling, she parked close to where he stood with several people in business attire. One of them a strikingly attractive woman about his sister's age.

Raquel, she guessed.

Had Betty and the other women been right?

Did Nora need to do a better job of looking after her man?

If she could even call Zane her man, that was. Since they still had no formally defined relationship. Broach or not.

Her heart accelerating as Zane strode toward her, Nora turned to Liam, said, "This will take just a minute, honey." Then turned off the engine and got out of the car.

"I wasn't expecting you."

He wasn't really glad to see her, either, Nora noted, standing next to the passenger door, in full view of her infant son.

"You're right." She wet her lips. "I should have called."

His gaze softened. "That's not what I meant." He stepped closer. "Is everything okay?"

"Yes." She swallowed around the parched feeling in her throat. "I'm just here because…" She walked around to the cargo area and opened it up. "The residents of Laramie Gardens wanted me to bring you this." She handed over the small prelit and already-decorated two-foot tree.

For a second, Zane was speechless.

As was she.

"Wow," he said finally.

Trying not to look as embarrassed as she felt, Nora continued, "They knew you hadn't put up a tree when you last talked with them, so they wanted to be sure you had something. As you can see, this decoration is designed to be set on a tabletop. And it's artificial, so you can pack it away and use it year after year, if you like."

Zane held it in front of him like a trophy. "I'll have to thank them when I see them."

Nora stepped back on shaking legs, chastising herself all the while. "Okay, then…"

"Nora." He caught her arm and swung her back around. Their glances met and held for several long beats.

Frowning, he inclined his head at the activity behind him. "I can't explain any of this just yet."

Of course he was shutting her out. Again. His time here was almost up. "You don't have to."

His eyes said he disagreed.

Regret sharpened the ruggedly handsome lines of his face. "I also can't do anything with you and Liam tonight."

"I wasn't expecting you to." A total lie. She had actually been counting on spending the evening together. Just Zane, her and Liam.

"I will be at the Ugly Sweater contest tomorrow, though."

Feeling her heart break a little more, her Christmas spirit diminish, Nora forced a bracing smile and said, "I'll see you then."

"IT'S NOT TOO late to enter the Ugly Sweater competition," Nora told Mr. Pierce the following afternoon. She had just learned the former bookseller was one of the few residents at Laramie Gardens not participating.

"I've got a hot glue gun in my office, a few extra red and green sweaters and all sorts of decorations. We could do *A Christmas Carol* theme. A likeness of Scrooge…" she teased. "Or something from any other holiday-themed novel you like."

"Thank you, dear, but I'm doing my best not to vary from my new routine. I want to be on track when my daughter, Lynn, visits."

Instead of the one leather-bound classic with clasp he typically carried, today he had two. *Treasure Island* and *Great Expectations*.

"I think I'd rather do a little more research on improving memory on my computer, and then rest. But if

I'm feeling up to it, I'll join the festivities in time for the judging," he promised.

Aware that was the best she was going to get, Nora told him, "Okay. But just so you know, if you change your mind, my offer to help you make a last-minute entry is good right up until the time of the contest..."

She went down the hall, checking in on residents. Clandestine activity abounded for the rest of the day, with final costume tweaking being done. And everywhere she went, one question was put to her—would Zane be competing, too?

"He promised he would," Nora said over and over, not really sure now that he would show up. Especially if whatever it was that was so important was still going on at the No Name ranch.

"Have you seen his ugly sweater?" Betty wanted to know.

No, and she had to admit, if he had found time to prepare one, she was a little curious.

"What time is he arriving?" Buck Franklin asked.

She had no idea about that, either, since she hadn't had so much as a text message from him after seeing him at his ranch. Probably because he didn't want her to ask any more questions he couldn't—or maybe just wouldn't—answer.

On the other hand, he always had been a man of his word. A man of honor.

"Hopefully he'll be here by the time it starts, at four o'clock," Nora said.

"I'm sure he'll surprise us," Wilbur Barnes said.

So was Nora. No matter what happened.

But she had no idea just how much, until Zane walked through the door.

Chapter Fourteen

The first thing Nora realized as the handsome warrior strode toward her was that she never should have doubted Zane's willingness to participate once he had declared the three of them "all in."

The second was that he was as much a rule breaker as ever.

The base sweater was a worn-to-the-point-of-ruin camouflage design with olive green leather elbow patches. Strands of multicolored blinking Christmas lights had been duct-taped to the sleeves, back and chest. The battery-pack that fueled them was attached to a wide black vinyl belt—that was also duct-taped to the sweater. Completing the ensemble was a bucket hat in the same camouflage green, with reindeer antlers popping up on either side of his head, double strands of mistletoe dangling from them.

It was, Nora noted with a mixture of exasperation and relief, exactly what they needed to break some of the too-serious tension in the room, as the time for competition neared.

Not that everyone agreed.

Betty leveled an accusing finger at Zane. "You're disqualified!" she said, clearly upset.

Zane didn't care.

Nor did Liam, whose eyes had lit up the moment he saw Zane striding toward them, Christmas lights blinking merrily. As the grinning lieutenant neared, Liam's face lit up even more. And then it began. A first, soft chuckle that swiftly evolved into a baby belly laugh, Liam's first.

And once Liam started laughing at Zane—who was by now laughing, too—he couldn't seem to stop. Nor could anyone else. The chuckles running through the room grew and grew until everyone was joining in the hilarity.

Betty frowned at Zane, the rule sheet still in her hand. "You're still disqualified," she fumed.

Zane winked at her playfully. He reached for Liam, who had his arms held out toward him. "As I should be," he murmured, moving quickly to catch the suddenly lurching Liam. "Hey there, little fella," he said, holding Liam against his chest and wrapping his other arm around Nora.

In front of everyone, he kissed her soundly on the lips. "Don't you look fetching, too," he murmured.

And in that instant, with tears of mirth still streaming down her face, Nora felt so much. Gratitude that Zane was there with them. Regret at all the time they had wasted over the years. Plus, a boundless enthusiasm for their future. No matter what happened from here on out, she knew what she wanted, and that was to be a part of Zane's life. And he, theirs.

"TELL ME THE TRUTH," Zane said, hours later, when the three of them had returned to her home and the exhausted Liam was tucked in bed. His ridiculous sweater and hat off, a navy one in its place, he finished lighting the fire in the hearth. He pivoted and sent Nora a knowing look. "You threw the competition on purpose."

Pretending to be indignant, Nora walked over to plug in

the Christmas tree lights. "What was wrong with Liam's and my sweaters?" She pointed to the back of the chair, where they were now displayed in all their eclectic glory.

She had sewn an adorable felt elf on the front of Liam's Christmas-green sweater and hot-glued a combination of fabric ornaments, and vinyl green-and-white-striped candy cane decals to the front of her red one.

"Uh-huh." Zane sank down beside her on the sofa.

Nora grinned and snuggled close. There was no use pretending she wasn't completely smitten with the two men in her life. "Okay, I confess that I simply wanted Liam to look cute. Otherwise, he would have had way too unfair an advantage."

Zane chuckled, recalling, "He almost won it with that belly laugh."

The thought of which still brought a sheen of happy tears to Nora's eyes. "His very first, by the way," she pointed out.

And it had all been because of Zane.

So much that was good this holiday season was because of him...

Zane stroked the back of her hand with his fingertips. "I'm glad I got to see that," he said tenderly.

"So am I." She turned her palm up, so it was facing his. "It was a special moment," she confessed softly. Made all the more special because Zane had been there, too. Marveling at how well they had always fit together—as if they were meant to be—she looked down at their entwined hands. "But it was good Miss Isabella walked away with the grand prize."

The handpainted holiday collage attached to the front of the former art teacher's Christmas-red sweater had been outrageously funny and loud, with colors clashing, yet somehow sweetly sentimental at the same time.

He nodded. "It's amazing how much she has perked up since Thanksgiving."

"Amazing how happy a lot of us are. I just wish Mr. Pierce hadn't been so blue tonight."

Zane recollected with concern, "He barely looked up from whatever he was doing on his computer tablet."

Nora sighed. "I think he may have been a little confused, too." She and the other nurses had noticed that happening more and more as the week had progressed, despite the new multitherapy regimen the older gentleman was on.

She forced herself to be optimistic. "Dr. Wheeler is coming in tomorrow morning to see him, so hopefully that will help."

"I'm sure it will." Keeping his dark silver gaze locked with hers, he stroked a comforting hand down her thigh. "So what else is on your mind?"

Nora swallowed around the rising lump in her throat, wondering if she was going to be able to find the nerve to do what she really wanted, and propose they craft a happily-ever-after. Whatever that looked like to him.

Married.

Engaged.

Or simply committed to each other, in their hearts and souls, from here on out. "I did want to talk to you about something important."

"Okay," he said softly.

She inhaled deeply. "Us."

The width of his smile etched grooves on either side of his mouth. He looked deep into her eyes with all the affection she had ever wanted and hoped to see. "We'll get to that before I leave again," he said soberly, "I promise you that. But right now—" one hand on her spine, he drew her even closer "—what I want more than anything is to make up for the time we lost this week. Because I missed you, Nora, so much…"

His lips fastened over hers and just that quickly all her worries fled. He kissed her in a way that had her senses spinning and her heart soaring.

The next thing she knew he was tossing one of the throws and several pillows on the floor before the fire and guiding her to the bed he made for them. Passion swept through her as he stretched out beside her.

She moaned softly as he clasped her to him and eased a hand beneath her shirt. He kissed her slow and deep, angling his head to get more of her, even as his clever hands moved upward and the fastening of her bra came undone.

She smiled as his palms came around to her breasts, slipping beneath the silk of her bra and stroking her nipples. A slow, warm heat began to fill her as they kissed hungrily, arching into each other, his rock-hardness a seduction in and of itself.

Her hands slipped beneath the hem of his sweater, too, finding the sleek muscles and satin warmth of his skin. He felt so good. So masculine. So right.

They felt so right.

"I want you," she murmured, against his lips.

"I want you, too." The wicked light in his eyes igniting all her erogenous zones, he sat up. Removed his sweater. She sat up and removed hers.

He pulled her onto his lap, so she was facing him, her arms encircling his neck. The clothing still between them was maddening. "Our jeans…"

"We'll get there. Promise…" And then his lips were on hers in a frenzy of wanting. Making her reckless, making her need, the powerful muscles of his chest abrading the softness of her breasts.

And still they kissed. Caresses pouring out of them. Feeling building. Desire exploding in liquid heat. Until unable to stand it any longer, they undressed the rest of the way, found protection and joined each other on the blanket before the fire.

She lifted her hips, her yearning every bit as fierce and all-encompassing as his. The hard length of him pressed into her, slowly, sensually. Hands sliding beneath her hips, lifting her, holding her still. Forcing her to submit to the hopelessly erotic, endless strokes. Deep, then shallow, then deep again.

All the while, their lips clung together, seducing, surrendering. Driving each other to the brink. Until all was lost in a perfect storm of wanting. Needing. Giving. Taking. And there was nothing but the heart and soul of that moment in time, nothing but the two of them. The earthshaking pleasure and the never-ending bliss, the perfection of the present, the sweet hope of the future.

He felt it, too.

It was clear in the way he gathered her close afterward, pressing kisses in her hair, along her temple, her jawline. The way they sagged against each other, spent and breathless. So safe and protected, their connection so strong and so right it felt unbreakable.

Until finally, he captured her lips in another hot, euphoric kiss, then lifted his head and gazed into her eyes, murmured softly, "I want you to know, Nora. There is only one woman on this earth for me. And it's you." His voice roughened even as his gaze grew unbearably fervent. "It's always been you…"

It wasn't the same thing as saying he was in love with her, but it was the closest he had ever come.

She celebrated that.

Heart swelling with all that she felt in return, Nora

admitted just as fervently, "You're the only man for me, too." And for the moment, maybe even forever, that would have to be enough.

"So you're going to be at the West Texas Warriors Assistance this morning," Nora said, as she and Zane bundled Liam up and headed out the door to her minivan.

He nodded. "They have a Job Finder session I want to sit in on."

Which meant what? Nora wondered. He was looking for a job? Thinking about looking for a job? Or searching for a reason not to try and find a job outside active duty military? There was no clue on his handsome face.

He flashed a grin. "Try not to miss me too much, okay?" he teased.

She wrinkled her nose right back at him, glad they already had plans to see each other for dinner. She saluted him sharply. "And you do the same, Lieutenant!"

Fortunately for Nora, it was slated to be a very busy day at Laramie Gardens. Which meant their time apart would pass quickly.

A good thing, given how much matchmaking she encountered when she reported for duty.

"Where is that handsome fella of yours?" Miss Mim teased while setting out boxes of undecorated sugar cookies.

Betty added colored frostings and sparkling sugar to the workstations set up in the dining room. "Not with Raquel, I hope."

Miss Sadie put in her two cents. "You have to keep an eye on your man, Nora!"

"As it happens he is with other ex-military personnel this morning," Nora said, as she passed out morning medications to those who required them.

"If I were you I'd get a ring on his finger, pronto," Miss Patricia said.

"Let him know you're serious," Miss Isabelle chimed in helpfully.

I tried last night, Nora thought, in silent frustration, *but Zane didn't let me get very far...*

Aware she'd have to be a lot more proactive if she wanted to get what she wanted out of their renewed relationship, Nora said wryly, "Thanks for the advice, ladies." She propped her hands on her hips, and assumed a total taskmaster stance. "Now, can we get cracking on decorating those sugar cookies we were going to send to the community caroling event at the town square?"

Chuckles abounded.

And there were some sympathetic looks, too.

The women at Laramie Gardens knew Nora well enough to know they had struck a nerve with their teasing. Albeit, unintentionally.

Fortunately, she still had more medication to pass out and a patient to get ready for an on-site medical appointment.

"You want me to wait in your office?" Mr. Pierce asked.

Nora paused while the older gentleman got comfortable, then handed him the insulated mug of green tea she'd been carrying for him. "Just for a few minutes. Dr. Wheeler is reviewing your records as we speak. As soon as he's done, he and I will confer, and then we'll bring you in."

Mr. Pierce set his leather-bound copy of *A Christmas Carol* and computer tablet on his lap. "Doc's got to be very busy with Christmas so close at hand."

Was it her imagination or was Mr. Pierce looking a

little manic this morning? "I think everyone is this time of year."

Mr. Pierce rubbed the elaborate buckle clasp on his book. "The weatherman said a cold front is coming in!"

Nora smiled. Moving to tidy up her office, she hung her coat on the hook behind the door, her purse on the one next to it, Liam's fleece hoodie on a third. "I heard."

He crossed his legs, then uncrossed them. "I also read that it'll be below freezing tonight, with a possibility of snow on Christmas Eve!"

Nora had heard less than a 10 percent chance. Still… "Wouldn't that be wonderful," she said, opening the blinds, so Mr. Pierce could see the people coming and going from the parking lot outside. Her red minivan that he had so admired gleamed in the winter sunshine.

He nodded vigorously. "Your son would love it. So will Lynn."

"They would." Spying her keys on the desk, Nora slipped them into the outside pocket on her purse.

"But it could hurt last-minute business for the retailers," Mr. Pierce predicted.

True. "Or encourage them to buy early!"

He grinned. "The holidays have always been a particularly busy time for booksellers. Including Esther and me."

Aware Mr. Pierce hadn't been this chatty in a long time—if ever—Nora straightened a stack of Welcome folders on her desk. "I remember," she said fondly. The Book Nook had been a treasure trove of gifts during the holidays. The married owners were a delight.

Mr. Pierce settled back in his chair and sipped his tea. "I want Lynn to have a very nice Christmas, too."

It was good he was focused on his daughter and her upcoming visit. Those plans would help keep him grounded. "I know she's excited," Nora said. The actress had already phoned to request that she and her father be allowed to eat at least one meal in the private dining room.

Mr. Pierce opened up his tablet. "I probably should make up a list," he said, as if anxious to get going. "I still have a lot to do to get ready for Christmas."

Didn't they all?

"Then I'll leave you to it." Nora shut the door quietly behind her and went down the hall to the conference room, where Dr. Wheeler was just finishing reviewing the files Nora had set in front of him.

"You're right." The physician looked up from the notes he had been making. "The time frame fits. But you and I have both done extensive research on possible drug interactions in this case. There's no documented evidence that the new antihistamine Mr. Pierce started taking after his move to New York City last summer could be causing his intermittent disorientation and memory issues."

But there was no documented evidence that it wasn't, Nora thought. Quietly, she persuaded, "It's only been on the market a year. Maybe there just isn't enough data yet for it to show up. Or maybe the new drug is fine on its own, but when it's combined with the particular blood pressure and cholesterol medications Mr. Pierce takes, there's an interaction. Or maybe for most people there is no negative side effect, even with that particular combination, but for him there is."

Dr. Wheeler steepled his hands in front of him. "You want to take him off the new potentially troublesome medication and put him back on his previous allergy medicine?"

Eager to get her fellow clinician on board, Nora nodded. "It's the only way to eliminate the new medication as being the culprit."

Dr. Wheeler closed the file. "Okay. Let's go see him."

Together, they walked down the hall.

Nora's office door was open.

Unfortunately, Mr. Pierce was not where she had left him. His travel mug of green tea, tablet and leather-bound copy of *A Christmas Carol* were also gone. "Maybe he went back to his suite," she said.

But Mr. Pierce wasn't there, either. Nor was he in the community room. The music room. The dining hall, or anywhere else they could fathom. In fact, they realized quickly, he wasn't anywhere on the premises, inside or out.

Beginning to panic, Nora called the Laramie County sheriff's department, and then Zane.

Both arrived within minutes.

Deputy Kyle McCabe strode in with several fellow officers. Zane and a whole cadre of ex-military followed.

Zane went straight to Nora and wrapped his arm around her shoulders. "We'll find Mr. Pierce," he promised.

But would it be in time? Nora wondered, distraught. "His brown leather jacket and fedora are still in the closet in his room. Which means all he has on is his flannel shirt and corduroy trousers."

And with it being around thirty-four degrees outside, hypothermia was a real concern for the eighty-five-year-old.

"How long do you think he's been gone?" Deputy McCabe asked.

Nora consulted her watch. "Thirty minutes, at most."

Zane speculated, "If he's on foot, he can't have gone far."

What if he wasn't in his right mind? "He could be confused."

"Is there anything else missing?" Deputy Kyle Mc-Cabe asked.

"Like what?" Nora asked.

"Your minivan," Zane said.

Nora rushed to the front of the building.

Sure enough, the space where she had parked was empty.

She dashed back to her office. Her purse was still there where she had left it, with her coat on the hook by the door. The exterior pocket was unzipped. She groaned. "My keys are gone, too."

Zane sobered all the more. "If he was confused, he might have thought he was driving his own vehicle."

Betty joined them. "He was talking about Esther at breakfast, and…well, it almost sounded as if he thought she were still here with us…"

Darrell Enlow joined them. "He asked me where I thought the best place in the county was to find a live tree if you wanted to cut it down yourself. I said I didn't know. I hadn't done it in years."

Miss Patricia said, "He also said something about getting his favorite Christmas ornaments out of storage."

"When I left him, he was making a list of things he still had left to do to get ready for Christmas," Nora added.

"So he's probably out running errands," Zane said.

Kyle took down the license plate of Nora's minivan, then issued a Silver Alert. "Two patrol cars are canvassing the town limits as we speak. No one has caught sight of him yet."

"We can't just stay here and do nothing." Nora wrung her hands.

"And we're not going to," Zane reassured her.

Ten minutes later, Zane and Kyle had worked together

to come up with a plan. The sheriff's department would canvass the far-flung roads and outlying areas, looking for Nora's minivan. The ex-military volunteers would cover all the businesses in town, going door to door to see if anyone had come in contact with Russell Pierce since he'd left Laramie Gardens.

Meanwhile, Miss Mim would work with all the residents to come up with any additional clues about what Mr. Pierce might be attempting to do to get ready for the holiday. And Zane and Nora would visit some of the more obvious places. His former bookstore, as well as the home where he used to live with Esther and Lynn.

"I should have seen this coming," Nora lamented, as they rushed outside to Zane's pickup truck.

He slanted her a glance, not about to baby her. "We can go through a debriefing of all the mistakes that were made later. Right now, let's just concentrate on finding Mr. Pierce."

Unfortunately, he wasn't at the bookstore he had once owned. The local storage facility hadn't seen him on the premises, either. And no one seemed to even be at the home Esther and Russell Pierce had once owned.

Undeterred, Zane peered around the side of the house into the backyard. Pointed. The door to the shed was wide open.

He and Nora hurried across the yard.

Inside, everything was neatly arranged except the garden tools area. Several of those looked like they had been picked up and thrown down. Zane said, "What do you want to bet he's after a Christmas tree he plans to cut himself?"

"Maybe Miss Mim or the other ladies might know where," Nora said. While she called Laramie Gardens and got the location of the most popular cut-it-yourself

Christmas tree farm years ago, as well as several others, Zane contacted all the military men and Kyle McCabe.

Frowning, he got off the phone, "My brother Garrett has enlisted everyone over at West Texas Warrior Assistance to continue canvassing the town, so I'm moving all my guys out into the countryside. Because it's possible Mr. Pierce got turned around if he's out there, we're going to cover every road. It'd be easier if we had air power, but the sheriff's department's one chopper still isn't available—it's on loan to another county sheriff's department for an ongoing search and rescue. Meantime, Kyle's trying to get a hold of Wade McCabe to see if they can borrow his."

"Of all the times to be shorthanded!" Nora fumed.

Zane looked like he wanted to say something, then closed his mouth. He guided her quickly back to his pickup truck. "Do you have directions for where you want to check first?"

"I do."

His jaw set. "Then let's move it."

It took them eighteen minutes to reach the location of what had once been the most popular Christmas tree farm, fifty years before. A rough-hewn property just east of Lake Laramie that had long ago gone to seed. "Now what?" Nora asked in frustration. "There's no way my minivan could cut through that much underbrush."

Zane drove a little farther down the country road. "Which is maybe why it's parked there." He pulled up beside Nora's vehicle.

The minivan's motor was turned off but the driver door had been left oddly ajar, the keys inside. While Zane quickly made the call to let the others know the vehicle had been found, the general area of Mr. Pierce's whereabouts pinpointed, Nora leaped out of the cab to peer inside the minivan.

Mr. Pierce's tablet was on the passenger seat along with his travel mug of tea and the leather-bound *A Christmas Carol*. Only this time, the buckle was undone.

"Help is on the way," Zane reported. He grabbed a pair of binoculars from his glove compartment and climbed on the bed of his pickup truck.

"Do you see him?" she asked Zane.

He scanned the wooded terrain. "Not yet. What color shirt was he wearing? Do you remember?"

"Green and brown plaid shirt, brown pants."

Zane groaned.

Nora knew how he felt. Mr. Pierce might as well have been wearing camouflage gear.

She grabbed the fleece blanket she always kept in her car, in winter, just in case of emergencies. The tea thermos—which still had a little bit of liquid in it. Then, on impulse, the book.

As she picked it up, it fell open. From the compartment formed by cutaway pages, a small white plastic bottle tumbled out and rolled across the seat. She bent to pick it up, and gasped at what it was.

"Problem?" Zane said.

Nora nodded and swiftly took off the cap, realizing it was empty. "A big one," she confirmed gravely, her panic turning to dread.

"Hey," Zane said, before she had time to explain, "I think I've got him in my sights! Yep! That's him, all right." He jumped down from the bed of the pickup.

Nora followed him through the heavy brush, into the woods. One hundred yards later, they encountered Mr. Pierce. The older gentleman was seated next to a gorgeous pine tree, an ax and a small tree saw, on the ground next to him. Seeing them, he pointed to the faint cut marks on the base of the tree trunk. "Had to stop and rest a minute," he explained, shivering.

"Understandable," Zane said.

Nora nodded. "I'm so glad we found you." Nora knelt and felt his skin. It was pale and cool to the touch. Hypothermia was definitely setting in. She wrapped the blanket about his shoulders.

"But I'm going to have to g-g-get going again soon." Mr. Pierce tried to rise on his own, failed. "Esther and Lynn will be expecting me to b-bring home a Christmas tree for them to decorate."

Zane knelt next to Mr. Pierce. He caught Nora's glance and understood well her concern. "Not to worry, sir. I'll take care of that. In the meantime, we have to warm you up a bit."

"Sounds g-good," Mr. Pierce said feebly, shivering all the harder. "It appears I forgot my coat…"

"And to speed things up," Zane continued, catching Nora's panicked look, seeming to realize that there was no time to wait for an ambulance to get all the way out there, "I'm going to carry you." He lifted Mr. Pierce in his strong arms, stood, and made his way deliberately through the brush.

Mr. Pierce chuckled feebly. "This is a first."

"Not for me," Zane joked right back, all macho alpha male. "It's how us military guys work out."

This time they all laughed.

Tears of worry and relief blurring her eyes, Nora grabbed the tools and led the way to safety.

Chapter Fifteen

"Are you angry with me?" Mr. Pierce asked Nora several hours later, when he had been moved out of the emergency room and into a regular hospital room. "You have every right to be."

Zane walked in with the belongings she had requested him to get from Laramie Gardens. He stood next to her, reminding her they were a team—and a very good one. "Concerned is more like it," Nora clarified.

She removed the stack of leather-bound books from the bag Zane carried. Opened the buckle on each one and removed a plastic over-the-counter pill bottle from each.

"Clever place to hide things," Zane observed.

"And safe, since no one reads the classics anymore," Mr. Pierce returned facetiously.

Aiding Zane in the attempt to get Mr. Zane to confide in them, she asked gently, "Do you want to tell us what this is all about?"

Mr. Pierce sighed. "I've been working on improving my memory. So in addition to eating almonds and drinking green tea, I've also taken a lot of all-natural supplements like herbs and vitamins."

"Every day?"

"Pretty much, when I can remember. I've tried them

all, alone or in combination. And before you ask, I kept it quiet because I knew not everyone would approve."

Especially the medical staff. "Did you keep any record of these trials?" Nora asked as Zane arched a brow in her direction.

Mr. Pierce pointed to his forehead. "Just up here."

"But it's been pretty regular since—?" she prodded.

"I moved to New York City to be with Lynn and had troubled getting acclimated. They had a health food store down the block from her apartment, and I went there."

Zane inched closer to Nora. "Did your daughter know this?"

"Lynn would have worried if she knew I needed assistance recalling things. So I didn't tell her I'd started taking supplements to boost my memory and sharpen my concentration skills."

"Or your doctors, either," Nora guessed.

He shrugged.

Nora pushed on. "Was this before or after you switched antihistamines?"

Mr. Pierce thought a moment. "A couple of weeks after, I guess."

His elbow bumping up against hers, Zane asked, "Were you having trouble staying focused before the switch in allergy medication?"

Mr. Pierce shook his head. "No. It was after that, I started forgetting things. And then, after that I added the natural remedies to counter the effects of aging." He began to look almost as upset as Nora and Zane felt. Glancing from one to another, he said, "Was that a mistake?"

And then some, Nora thought. Basking in the support Zane offered, she went on kindly, "Here's the thing, Mr. Pierce. These herbal supplements are all anticholinergic.

Which means they inhibit activity of the neurotransmitter acetylcholine, which plays an essential role in memory and cognitive function. When you combine them with the medications you already take to control your blood pressure and lower cholesterol, they can produce mild cognitive impairment. Or dementia and Alzheimer-like symptoms."

Mr. Pierce turned pale. "So you think this may have been the problem all along?" he asked, aghast. "The combination of my new antihistamine and the natural supplements I added?"

Nora, who had already talked to his geriatric specialist on the phone, nodded. "Dr. Wheeler and I are betting on it."

Mr. Pierce smiled. "So to get better, all I have to do is…?"

"Switch back to your old allergy medication and stop taking any and all unauthorized supplements. Herbal or otherwise."

Nora and Zane talked to Mr. Pierce a few more minutes. Reassured him he would be getting out of the hospital the following day in plenty of time to enjoy Christmas Eve with his daughter, Lynn.

Together, they headed out into the hall. Taking advantage of the momentary quiet, Nora took Zane's hand in hers. "Have I told you how much I appreciate everything you did for us today?" she murmured. She rose up on tiptoe and brushed her lips across his. "You were quite the hero."

He laced an arm about her waist and pulled her closer. "Haven't you heard?" he quipped, kissing her back. "Being a hero is my full-time job."

"How well I know that," she replied, dancing him

back into the hidden alcove opposite the elevators and kissing him again.

In fact, she was beginning to see the two were intrinsically interlinked.

The doors slid open.

One of the nurses who'd taken care of Mr. Pierce in the ER stepped out.

"And here I thought there wasn't enough mistletoe to go around," she teased.

Zane and Nora exchanged baffled glances. "Ah, we don't have any mistletoe," he said.

Although that, too, could be remedied, Nora thought happily.

The nurse winked. "And you don't appear to need it, either!"

THAT EVENING, THE RESIDENTS of Laramie Gardens threw a party to thank everyone who had aided in the search for Mr. Pierce. While Zane made the rounds, with Liam in a BabyBjörn strapped to his wide chest, Nora helped the women put out the holiday spread for the guests.

But even as they worked, no one could keep from looking at the soldier in the center of the room. Zane was just so handsome and charismatic, Nora thought on a wistful sigh. So big and manly he made her feel like a woman every time she saw him.

Miss Sadie followed Nora's surreptitious glance. "You have to nail that hunk of burnin' love down and get a ring on your finger before he leaves again!" she murmured, as she put out the cranberry molds.

"I second that!" Betty chimed in, adding a fresh tray of brisket sliders to the buffet.

Miss Patricia handed Nora a sprig of mistletoe and a CD of an old but cherished copy of *Andy Williams Christ-*

mas Favorites. "Just in case you need something to set the mood." She winked.

Nora didn't think she and Zane needed any help setting their mood. They couldn't keep their hands off each other.

Miss Isabelle patted her arm. "Times like this, dear, a woman needs to use every tool in her arsenal."

Nora put the last of the side dishes and salads out. "I'll remember that," she opined drily, already thinking how much fun it would be to recount this conversation to Zane later.

"In fact…" She picked up a tray of cookies and headed for Zane, who was now surrounded by a group of ex-military and sheriff's deputies. She turned and winked at her group of cheerleaders. "I'll get started right now."

As she neared him, she heard Deputy Kyle McCabe say, "…appreciate how quickly you were able to jump into the action today…organize others…a real asset… The sheriff's department could really use you."

That's what Nora had been hearing, too.

Although sadly Zane had told her in no uncertain terms he wasn't interested in doing a job that included handing out traffic tickets…

She stopped to offer refreshment to Buck Franklin and Kurtis Kelley. As the residents helped themselves to cookies, another military guy said, "I heard via the grapevine they've been doing everything possible to get you to reenlist."

Zane shrugged, his back still to her, so she could not read the expression on his face. "That's always the case," he said mildly.

Darrell Enlow walked up to join the group, adding, "Despite what Nora said, she will support you."

Nora's heart stuttered in her chest, listening raptly

to every word. Kyle McCabe, who had known her since childhood, agreed. "She'll wait for you," he promised.

Except in the past, she thought guiltily, she hadn't really done that. She and Zane had always eventually gotten back together, but there had been an awful lot of heartache and loneliness in between their hookups.

And that remained one of her biggest life regrets.

They had wasted so much time.

So many opportunities to be together emotionally, if not physically.

As she ventured even closer, Zane's older brother, Garrett, elbowed Zane lightly in the ribs. "And speaking of the gal who's got your heart…"

But did she? Nora wondered, thinking of all Zane had been up to recently that he hadn't actually confided in her.

On the other hand, there were things she hadn't gotten around to telling him, either. Things she still needed to say.

As if sensing her presence behind him, Zane swung around to face Nora. He gave her a slow, affectionate once-over, seeming to see how completely exhausted she was, while as usual he still had tons of energy left. He looked down at the yawning baby strapped to his chest. "I think this little guy's about had it." He reached over to take her hand, his expression radiating the tender devotion she so adored. "Ready to go home?"

She knew it was selfish, but she wanted her alone time with him. Especially now that their days together were dwindling. "Yes," she said, smiling back and gearing up for all that yet had to be said. "I am."

Half an hour later, Liam was in bed, fast asleep, and Zane and Nora were finally settled before the fire.

She had been waiting for this moment for weeks now,

even thinking she might dare to propose to him. Yet suddenly she was a bundle of nerves. Worried it all might go awry.

He clasped her shoulders lightly and drew her into the curve of his big strong body. "You okay?" he asked, pressing a kiss on the top of her head.

Nora inhaled deeply and tried to calm down.

Why was he looking at her like that? As if he half expected her to do what she always did when their time together approached an end, and break up with him tonight?

"Why wouldn't I be?" she countered.

He chuckled and stroked a thumb down her cheek. "Maybe because you looked like you were getting some vigorous advice on how to handle your man from the Laramie Gardens ladies tonight."

Perceptive, as always. "You were getting the same kind of life coaching, from what I heard."

Zane inclined his head to the side, unperturbed. "Everyone means well."

Even as they push us together. "They do." Nora nodded.

"But…?" he prodded.

Knowing it was now or never, Nora sighed. Moving out of the cozy curve of his body, she perched on the edge of the sofa and pivoted to face him. Hands clasped together on her lap, she announced firmly, "We also need to talk. And we need to do it tonight."

ZANE WANTED TO tell Nora everything. She had no idea how badly. But only once it was all set. He lifted a staying hand. "I need a few more days, Nora." That was all he was asking.

They stared at each other.

She sighed and ran her hands through her hair. "Until after Christmas," she deduced unhappily.

Or sooner.

He wasn't quite sure.

So erring on the side of caution, he just said, "Yes."

Nora squared her slender shoulders deliberately and huffed out a breath. "No, Zane. You don't need more time before we talk about what's next for us."

"I don't?" he echoed in confusion.

Her slender body quivering with emotion, Nora drew a deep breath. "It's okay if you want to go back to your unit. I understand."

This was new, Zane thought. And not in a good way.

The tip of Nora's tongue snaked out to wet her lower lip. "You don't belong here in Laramie, Zane. And the truth is, you never have," she said, holding all the tighter to his hands. "You know it. I know it…"

He'd never seen her so overwrought or so incredibly, passionately, beautiful. He shifted her over onto his lap. Adjusted his posture to ease the pressure building at the front of his slacks and felt her begin to blissfully relax.

He rubbed his thumb across the soft dampness of her lower lip. Looked deep into her eyes. "Where do you see me?"

Nora wreathed one arm about his shoulders, splayed the other hand across the center of his chest. Her expressive brows lowering over her long-lashed eyes, she replied, "Where you have always belonged. With your unit in the Special Forces."

He stared at her, hardly able to believe she was pushing him away. The way she always did before any expected deployment.

Again.

He'd thought—hoped—with the connection they had forged, with Liam's help, that they had gotten past all that.

Still, he tried to give her the benefit of the doubt. "And here I thought I'd been making myself useful around here," he deadpanned.

For a second, Nora turned her glance away and the pink in her cheeks deepened. Her lips tightened. Slowly but surely, the walls around her heart began to go back up. With a contrite smile, she turned to look him in the eye. "That's the hell of it. You have. With the Laramie Gardens residents. The ex-military guys over at the WTWA. Liam. Me. Your family."

Her pretty sky blue eyes began to fill with tears. "We're all going to miss you terribly," she admitted, her lush lower lip quivering. "But we can't let our feelings dictate what you do or where you go." She withdrew herself from his embrace, stood. And walked over to the fireplace. She fingered the less-than-pleasing photo of Liam, with Santa displayed there.

As a reminder that life wasn't always perfect? he wondered.

Swallowing she turned back to face him. "And I know you realize it, too. Even if you're not ready to admit it to me just yet."

His emotions in turmoil, too, he stood. "How do you figure that?"

She waved an airy hand. "It's why you've been putting off having any kind of serious talk until after Christmas Day. The same goes for your family. It's why you are preparing to sell the ranch your father left you."

He joined her at the mantel. The heat emanating from the hearth was nothing compared to the fire roiling deep inside his gut.

He lounged beside her. "How long since you deduced all this?"

To his increasing frustration, his sarcasm seemed lost on her.

Turning to face him, she angled her chin at him and continued blithely, "I realized what was going on the day I delivered the tabletop tree to the No Name."

He lifted his brow, wordlessly urging her to go on.

"You had the most knowledgeable real estate broker in Laramie County out there. A group of surveyors. Sage's friend Raquel, from Dallas."

He shook his head, hoping that would clear it. "So?"

"You didn't want to talk about any of it to me, Zane. You still don't."

He rubbed at the tension gathering in the back of his neck, said wearily, "I had my reasons, Nora." *And I still do.*

"Yes," she said, determined to keep her blinders on. Her lower lip slid out in a delicious pout. "Because you didn't want our latest hookup to end the way it always does just yet."

"Hookup," he echoed in shock, wondering how this conversation could get any more disappointing.

"Or fling or reconnection. Whatever you want to call it."

Semantics weren't what was bothering him here.

"How about Part Two in Our Never Really Ending Relationship?"

His sardonic humor was completely lost on her.

She propped her hands on her hips. Clearly exasperated, said, "That's exactly what I'm trying to tell you, Zane. Our relationship with each other doesn't have to end."

She came close enough to take him in her arms again. Said with fierce finality, "I want to be on-again with you from here on out. I want you to know that Liam and I will be here, waiting for you and supporting you, no matter how long or how often you're gone."

NORA WASN'T SURE why her matter-of-fact declaration was being met with such stunned silence. She'd expected the knowledge that they would be here for him from this day forward would make him incredibly happy.

Instead, he looked stunned. And wary. Too wary for comfort.

"And you'll be content with that?" he asked quietly, keeping his physical distance in a way she hadn't expected. He rested an arm on the mantel. "Seeing each other only occasionally? Making do with what time the military gives us?"

Of course not! But she'd finally found a way to be there for him. To be as honorable and duty driven as he was, deep down. And most especially, to be able to nobly sacrifice the way he did. "I promise, from here on out, I'm going to be a good military…"

He frowned when she stumbled, trying to come up with the right word to categorize what they had yet to precisely define. "Girlfriend?" he asked mildly.

Was he angry? Hard to tell, but it certainly seemed so.

Aware this was all starting to go mysteriously awry, Nora swallowed. "I think—if you're asking—that I prefer the term *your woman*. Or *your significant other*. But—" she drew another deep breath, still floundering under his steady regard "—if you'd like to say something more contemporary, we could always call me your…um…*person*…?"

His expression maddeningly impassive, Zane folded his arms. His gaze sifted over her face before returning with slow deliberation to her eyes. "How about *love interest*? Would that work?"

Like she cared how others viewed them, she thought grumpily. Their relationship was theirs and theirs alone. She thought she had made that clear! Apparently not.

She moved toward him, hands outspread. Suddenly feeling as piqued and out of sorts as he looked. "Why are you so ticked off, anyway? I'm finally giving you what you always wanted from me, Zane! My unwavering, unconditional support."

His dark silver eyes narrowed. He turned and walked away from her. "With one foot out the door, of course."

Tensing anxiously, she followed. "I'm giving you your freedom instead of boxing you in, the way you always hated."

He swung around to square off with her once again. His jaw set. He stared at her long and hard, then shook his head. "I really thought things had changed between us."

Nora took him by the arms. "They have!"

His biceps were rock hard, resistant, beneath her compelling grip. "No," he countered sternly, "they haven't, Nora. My family. The guys in the unit. The fellows at Laramie Gardens and now, *even you*. You all have an opinion as to what I should do."

He stepped back and angled a thumb at the center of his chest.

Anger vibrated in the air between them. "And yet… as much as you proclaim to care for me…you've never once asked me what I want! Or what I think would be good for us."

He was twisting things, deliberately misinterpreting her actions, the way he always did whenever they got too close. Or he risked having *her* ask too much of *him*.

The heat of rejection pushed from her chest into her

face. She'd thought things were different, too. But were they, after all?

"I just did that," she retorted evenly.

He shook his head, regret etching the hard, uncompromising lines of his handsome face. "No, Nora, you made a huge *assumption* predicated on what you *thought* I was going to do between now and January 15, when my current enlistment ends. And you let me know you were okay with your expectation." He grimaced unhappily. "Especially now that you have your guard back up."

Nora dropped her hands as if she'd been stung. And to think, she'd been about to propose to this man! She stepped back, feeling as if the entire world were quaking beneath her feet.

Hurt filled her low tone. "That wasn't what I was doing!" Tears filled her eyes. She did her best to contain them.

He quirked a dissenting brow.

"I was finally being supportive in the best, the only way I know how," she continued, feeling utterly humiliated.

Even if he still had yet to be completely forthcoming with her. And maybe, she realized sadly, acutely aware of how he was still shutting her out, he never would be.

But once again, Zane didn't see it her way.

"No, Nora," he corrected bitterly, a muscle working in his jaw. "You were protecting your heart, once again. Valiantly pushing me out the door and out of your life— just in time for the first and only Christmas we've been blessed to actually spend together!" He turned on his heel and grabbed his coat. "And guess what? I'm going!"

Chapter Sixteen

"What's wrong, dear?" Miss Mim asked Nora on the morning of Christmas Eve.

Everything, Nora thought miserably. But wary of spoiling anyone else's holiday, Nora continued setting out small gift baskets at every seat in the dining hall. "What could be wrong? Mr. Pierce is safe and sound and celebrating the holiday with his daughter, Lynn." Plus, his medical mystery had been solved.

She nodded at the community room, which was filled with laughter and music.

"We've had children in and out all day, bringing gifts and spending time with residents as part of our new Adopt a Grandparent program."

A fact which had made Miss Isabella and others very happy.

"And we're set to have a wonderful holiday meal this evening, and another in the dining hall tomorrow afternoon."

Miss Mim moved behind Nora, adding poinsettia centerpieces. "Have you heard from your family?"

Nora and Miss Mim went back to the storage area to replenish their pushcarts.

"My mother and my sister, Davina, both called this morning to wish us a merry Christmas, and FaceTime with us a bit." Which had been the one-and-only really bright spot of her day thus far.

Miss Mim cast a fond look at Liam, who currently was nestled in Miss Patricia's arms while Miss Sadie entertained him with an impromptu puppet show. "What about Zane?"

Liam let out a belly laugh at the antics of the stuffed lamb and pig, which made everyone within earshot grin.

Aware the retired librarian was awaiting an answer, Nora helped her finish loading her cart with more centerpieces. "He has a family thing this evening."

Together, they pushed their carts back out into the dining hall. Miss Mim slanted her a glance. "Are you going?"

She had been. Until they'd quarreled. Now, given the way he'd stormed out on her, it didn't seem like a good idea at all. Nora worked hard to suppress a self-conscious blush. "I was invited," she informed truthfully.

"But are you attending?" the older woman pressed.

Nora only wished that were still possible. But not wanting to get into it, shrugged and murmured, "It depends on Liam." She smiled as her son yawned. "He's had a busy few days."

We all have.

And though Nora wished she could blame her fight with Zane on the fact they were both worn-out and dreading the end of their time together, she knew it was more than that.

She had given him every opportunity and he still didn't trust her enough to tell her the truth about his plans.

Mistaking the reason behind Nora's contemplative silence, Miss Mim patted her hand. "I'm sorry if the other ladies and I have given you too much advice," she said kindly, pausing to take a seat.

Nora did the same.

"It's just we don't want you to make our mistakes." Miss Mim shook her head. "Time passes so quickly. When you get to be our age, you realize how fleeting it is. How some opportunities only come once and even if we're wise enough *not* to squander them, the moments are fleeting anyway."

Sadly, Nora knew how true that was.

Zane had been in Texas for almost a month now, and it seemed like their time together had passed in an instant.

Quietly, the older woman insisted, "Whatever is keeping you and Zane apart can be fixed, Nora."

Could it?

She wondered.

"If only you're brave enough to open up your heart and try…"

ZANE WAS CHOPPING wood when Sage arrived at the No Name ranch, already dressed for the Lockharts' Christmas Eve celebration.

He wasn't surprised to see his meddlesome only sister arrive. Nor was he shocked at what she had to say, as she made her way carefully over the rough terrain. "I can't believe you blew it with Nora. Again."

"She's the one who pushed me out the door with both hands."

"Only because she had no clue what you've been up to for the past month. Face it. You made a mistake, not telling Nora what you were doing out here."

He had wanted to. Numerous times. But… "She set the rules, Sage." No more broken promises.

And since there had been no way he could guarantee how it would all work out, he'd had to ignore every romantic impulse he had and remain silent about that part of his future.

"It's not as if I didn't let her know how I felt about her and Liam a dozen other ways."

"Such as...?"

"I set up a little nursery out here for Liam."

"So she could spend the night with you."

He clenched his jaw. "So they both could spend the night out here." What he had hoped would be the start of many.

Sage shivered in the cold December air.

"I took steps to provide for them financially."

His sister persisted doggedly. "But did you tell her you love her?"

"She knows she's the only woman in the world for me."

"So you didn't mention love."

"Listen, Dear Abby..."

She propped her hands on her hips. "I know you think they are just words, Zane. But women need to hear them."

Zane found it hard to believe that Nora would have shoved him out the door over a few unsaid words. "We were more than that, Sage." At least he'd thought they were.

She lifted a brow. "More than love?"

Zane picked up a load of split logs and carried them toward the ranch house. He stacked them neatly on the porch, then went back for another half dozen. "I wanted things to work out."

"Really?" As determined as ever to make him see the wisdom of her words, Sage dogged his every step. "Because it looked to me like it wasn't just Nora who has had her doubts. You haven't been sure you could be happy with her, either."

Zane exhaled. Had he ever seen a gloomier Christmas Eve? He didn't think so.

"It's true." He carried the last of the split logs to the porch. "I've never been the kind of guy who could sit still for even a day."

Sage followed him inside. Watched as he washed up. "And now, thanks to all your very hard work putting together a very big endeavor in a very short time, you won't have to worry you'll get bored in Laramie County. Because every day is likely to be as different and challenging and important to everyone involved as the next."

Zane dried his hands. "Yeah—" he shrugged, discouragement flooding his soul "—but will any of it matter to Nora?"

Would it make her want what he wanted most of all?

Sage took him by the arms and forced him to look at her. "Listen to me, Zane," she said softly. "You're not the first couple to find yourself in a potentially heartbreaking situation. Nick and I went through the same thing."

Hard to imagine, they were so happy now. But what did he know about what had gone down between them? He'd been with his unit, overseas during most of the courtships of all four of his siblings.

Calmly, he pointed out what he did know. "You never disapproved of Nick's life work."

"But I worried I wouldn't fit into his life. And as it turns out—" Sage paused to let her words sink in "—he was just as worried about making me happy. We didn't know that, though, because we were so busy trying to keep it casual and hide what we were really thinking and feeling that we almost lost each other." Tears sparkled in her eyes. "We would have if we hadn't found the courage to tell each other what was in our hearts."

Zane inhaled deeply. "You're saying I should go to Nora?"

"And make it the merriest Christmas of all, by telling her all you've been doing behind the scenes to see that you will have the kind of future together that will make you-all blissfully happy."

As ZANE SHOWERED and got ready for the family party, he realized his sister was right. Mistakes had been made. Lots of them. But there was still time to fix everything.

And it had to be done in person.

As he was walking out the door, he saw a familiar red minivan coming up the drive. *Nora.* She was the last person he expected to see and the person he most wanted to connect with, too.

He stood, hands in his pockets, waiting, until the van stopped and Nora got out. She came toward him, her chin held high, her expression so resolute it set his heart to pounding.

He glanced inquiringly at the rear passenger seat.

"Liam is with your mother at the Circle H."

Which meant what? His mother had been involved in the last-minute matchmaking efforts, too? Or Nora and Liam intended to attend the party with him, after all?

Looking gorgeous as ever in a red wool coat, a white scarf wound around her neck, Nora met him at the top of the steps. "I wanted us to be able to talk without interruption."

Talking sounded good. But first...

Zane ushered her inside, out of the cold, and said, "Before we do that, I owe you an apology."

"For what?"

He exhaled roughly. "For overreacting...and for storming out."

He watched her unwind her scarf, then helped her off with her coat. Took off his own. Taking her by the hand, he led her over to the sofa.

"I thought about it," he told her as they sat down, knee to knee. Clasping her soft hands in his, he confided gruffly, "And I realize what you were trying to do, letting me know it was okay with you if I wanted to reenlist again. It was a big sacrifice."

Nora's lips curved ruefully. "Not enough of one." She clasped his hands tighter and looked intently into his eyes. "Because you were right, Zane. I decided your future for you because it was easier than facing my own issues."

This was a big admission.

And a startling one.

"Which are?" he asked, really wanting to understand.

"All my life I've equated love with loss, need with abandonment. And that mindset was even worse after my grandparents died." She choked up. "So I've tried really hard not to let or allow myself to be vulnerable with anyone."

He used his thumbs to wipe away the tears trembling on her lower lashes. "It wasn't just you putting up walls, Nora," he told her, wrapping his arms around her. "I've done the same thing."

She rested her forehead in the curve of his neck. Inhaled a shaky breath. "At least your reason was noble. Made out of honor and duty to your country."

Tucking a hand beneath her chin, he lifted her gaze to his. "In some respects, yes. But in others, it was done out of a fear of being boxed in, bored, restless." All the bane of his youth.

Nora looked at him long and hard. "And now?"

"I found a solution."

He released her and rose. Taking her by the hand, he led her over to his desk. "I didn't want to tell you until the dream became a reality. But now that it has…" He opened up a folder, handed her a blueprint and a business plan.

Nora studied both. Cheeks pinkening, she read in surprise. "Lockhart Search And Rescue?"

"Laramie County does not have a dedicated search and rescue team. Nor do any of the surrounding counties."

She nodded. "None of them have the budget for a service that is only needed part of the time. Which, as we found out with Mr. Pierce's situation this week, is a real problem."

"Right, because in an emergency, they're left to cobble together resources as best they can, sometimes from as far away as San Antonio or Dallas. And they pay exorbitant rates for them, too."

Nora's eyes lit up. "So there is a definite need," she said, beginning to understand.

Zane nodded, relieved to have this all out in the open. "One I plan to fill with ex-military, like me, who are skilled in search and rescue. I'll run it out of the No Name—which by the way will be rechristened with the name of the new business—and have help on-site available to be dispatched twenty-four hours a day, seven days a week for a seven-county radius."

Nora blinked in surprise. "So that's what's been going on out here?"

"Choppers don't come cheap. To get a small business loan, I had to come up with a comprehensive business plan and put my ranch up as collateral. To do that, I had to have the property appraised. Thanks to Sage's banker friend, Raquel, in Dallas, I got what we needed," he announced happily. "The loan was approved yesterday. The funds will be in place by the time I come back to Texas on January 15."

Hurt shimmered in her eyes. "Why didn't you tell me?" she asked, confused.

"I should have. I know that now."

"But while all this was going on...?"

Brusquely, he admitted, "I had promised you stuff before, then was unable to deliver on those vows. I didn't want to do that again."

Her pretty eyes lit with understanding, giving him the courage to go on.

He drew her all the way into his arms. "And to be honest, when I first came back to Laramie, I didn't know what I was going to be able to do here professionally."

To his relief, she understood that, too.

"*Until* I started talking to the people at the sheriff's, fire and EMS departments," he confessed, breathing in the sweet, womanly scent of her. "And realized just how little they had to offer me in the way of full-time work that matched my skills, and yet how deep their need went, too."

Nora nodded, smiling. "So the next time someone gets lost...or wanders off from a campsite..."

"It'll be Lockhart Search and Rescue that gets called."

She studied him a long moment. "You really want to do this?"

Contentment flowed through him. He brought her even closer. "I really do."

Nora lifted her lips to his. "Oh, Zane, I love you so much."

His heart swelled. "I love you, too." He kissed her softly, deeply. Then lifted his head, eager to spill the rest. Smiling, he said, "And that brings me to the second part of my plan to make this the best Christmas ever."

With her watching raptly, Zane produced a velvet box. She flipped open the lid and gasped at the gleaming platinum solitaire diamond inside.

"Marry me, Nora," he urged in a voice filled with all the affection he felt. "And let me be the husband and father you and Liam deserve. Let me make all your dreams come true."

Nora's pulse pounded with excitement and joy. This was the best Christmas present he could ever have given her! Better yet, a start to a new and wonderful life for them all. Happy tears spilling down her cheeks, she threw her arms around his neck, stood on tiptoe and gave him a resounding kiss, amplified by all the love and tenderness she felt in her heart. He really was all she had ever wanted and needed, and at long last she knew she was that for him, too.

"Yes, Zane," she murmured emotionally, basking in the love flowing freely between them, "yes!"

Epilogue

One year later

Looking gorgeous as ever, Nora stood ten feet back from the entrance to Lockhart Search and Rescue, sixteen-month-old Liam in her arms. A Christmas wreath looped over one shoulder, Zane moved the ladder beneath the iron archway. "You're going to have to tell me where you want it," he said.

Nora squinted, considering. "The center would be good."

"Cen', Daddy!" Liam shouted, pumping both his little arms.

Grinning at his son's helpfulness, Zane positioned the evergreen wreath with the red velvet bow. "Here?" he asked his two "helpers."

Nora tilted her head to one side, a cascade of chestnut hair spilled across her slender shoulder. "A little to the right," she said finally.

Trying not to be distracted by the new lushness of her curves—not an easy task—he obliged. "Here?"

She paused, then pursed her soft lips together in a very kissable pout.

But then, her lips were always kissable...

"Maybe slightly to the left," she said finally.

Zane moved it again.

"Another inch."

Not sure what she was going for—weren't they about to get off center now?—he again moved the wreath ever so slightly.

"Again. In the other direction."

Frowning, he did as asked.

"No," she corrected, sighing loudly, "back the other way!"

He turned and saw her peering at him mischievously. She laughed at the baleful expression he gave her.

"Actually," she said drily, "that's good right there."

He regarded her with comically exaggerated admonition. "It's good that's good." He waggled his brows teasingly. "Or we'd be switching places."

"Which would be a real problem since I'm not tall enough to reach that, even with the ladder."

He chuckled. "True."

"True, Daddy!" Liam echoed. Then at their looks of surprise, he pumped his little arms and let out a belly laugh that quickly had them laughing even more.

Finished fastening the decoration, Zane climbed back down and returned the ladder to the bed of his pickup truck.

Aware he had never been more content in his life, he moved to stand next to his family. Gazing down at Nora's lovely face, he asked, "How long before the activity buses from Laramie Gardens arrive?"

Nora consulted her watch. "Thirty minutes."

"How many times have they been out here?"

She wrinkled her nose. "I think this makes their tenth tour. But the residents never tire of seeing the equipment you use and talking with the guys and gals who work here, so…it's all good."

"It is all good." With a smile, he leaned down to kiss her. "Starting with the fact we're married."

"Agreed."

"Proud parents of one amazing child." He cast an adoring look at Liam, then reached down to pat her tummy. "With another on the way…"

Nora grinned, shifting the son they had both adopted over to his arms for holding. "I really agree there."

Wrapping an arm around her shoulders, while cuddling Liam on the right, he brought her in close to his left side. Brushed his lips across her temple. "I never imagined I could be as happy as I am now."

"Neither did I," Nora whispered back.

But they were.

Smiling, she predicted, "And the best is yet to come…"

* * * * *

Get 2 Free Books,

Plus 2 Free Gifts—

just for trying the Reader Service!

SPECIAL EXCERPT FROM

◆ HARLEQUIN®

Western Romance

*Amy Donovan has just fled an abusive marriage
with her infant son—straight into the arms of
Connor McCullough, the man she left behind.
With Christmas in the air in Forever, Texas,
can they find their way back to each other?*

Read on for a sneak preview of
A BABY FOR CHRISTMAS,
the next heartwarming installment of the
FOREVER, TEXAS *series*
by USA TODAY *bestselling author Marie Ferrarella.*

"I never knew you had a bit of a lawyer in you," Amy said.

"No lawyer. I'm just someone who had to raise three scrappy kids while trying to keep a ranch going and earning some sort of a profit. You learn how to put out potential fires before they get started," he told her with a wink.

"You do have a lot of skills," Amy said with unabashed admiration.

Connor had no idea what possessed him to look down into her incredibly tempting upturned face and murmur, "You have no idea."

Nor could he have said what spurred him on to do what he did next.

Because one minute they were just talking, shooting the breeze like two very old friends who knew one another well enough to finish each other's sentences, and then the next minute, somehow those same lips that were responsible for making those flippant quips had found their way to hers.

And just like that, with no warning, he was kissing her.

Kissing Amy the way he had always wanted to from perhaps the very first moment he had laid eyes on her all those years ago.

And the kiss turned out to be better than he'd thought it would be.

Way better.

It wasn't a case of just lips meeting lips, it was soul meeting soul.

Before Connor knew it, his arms had slipped around her, all but literally sweeping her off her feet and pulling her against him.

Into him.

The kiss deepened as he felt his pulse accelerating. He knew he shouldn't be doing this, not yet, not when she was still this vulnerable.

But despite his trying to talk himself out of it, it felt as if everything in his whole life had been leading to this very moment, and it would somehow be against the natural order of things if he didn't at least allow himself to enjoy this for a single, shimmering moment in time.

Don't miss A BABY FOR CHRISTMAS
by Marie Ferrarella, available December 2017
wherever Harlequin® Western Romance books
and ebooks are sold.

www.Harlequin.com

HWREXP1117

Looking for more satisfying love stories
with community and family at their core?

Check out **Harlequin® Special Edition**
and **Harlequin® Western Romance** books!

New books available every month!

CONNECT WITH US AT:

Harlequin.com/Community

Facebook.com/HarlequinBooks

Twitter.com/HarlequinBooks

Instagram.com/HarlequinBooks

Pinterest.com/HarlequinBooks

ReaderService.com

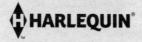

**ROMANCE WHEN
YOU NEED IT**

HFGENRE2017R

THE WORLD IS BETTER WITH

Romance

Harlequin has everything from contemporary, passionate and heartwarming to suspenseful and inspirational stories.

Whatever your mood, we have a romance just for you!

Connect with us to find your next great read, special offers and more.

f /HarlequinBooks

🐦 @HarlequinBooks

www.HarlequinBlog.com

www.Harlequin.com/Newsletters